The Doorkeepers

The Doorkeepers

Chris Curley

Oxford University Press
Oxford New York Toronto

Oxford University Press, Walton Street, Oxford OX2 6DP

Oxford New York Toronto
Delhi Bombay Calcutta Madras Karachi
Petaling Jaya Singapore Hong Kong Tokyo
Nairobi Dar es Salaam Cape Town
Melbourne Auckland

and associated companies in
Berlin Ibadan

Oxford is a trade mark of Oxford University Press

British Library Cataloguing in Publication Data
Curley, Chris
The doorkeepers
I. Title
813'.54 [J]

ISBN 0 19 271626 3

Typeset by Pentacor Ltd, High Wycombe, Bucks

Printed and bound in Great Britain by
Biddles Ltd, Guildford and King's Lynn

To Peter Specht

Contents

CHAPTER 1

A Shape of Things to Come

After the row over the Historic Doorknob, Paddy-last crept away to sulk. He went into the spare bedroom, a chilly and uninhabited place, and stood at the window there. Most of the neighbourhood lay before him, from Whites' empty house to Joyces' small cottage, and up the hill to Drumanaar's black silhouette. Paddy-last watched the evening shadows stretch and finally cover each hollow, hedge and hill. The waxing moon rose to glisten on the fresh snail paths and in the eyes of the night. Paddy saw each house light up, all except Whites'. The country house lights were self-contained and didn't diminish the greater night. Night creatures need no street lamps to show where fields begin or roads end.

Now the spare room was entirely dark, but Paddy-last was comfortably aware of his family in the rest of the house. Maybe they would worry about where he was, and be sorry that they had made such a fuss over the Historic Doorknob, and the window he had helped it to break. Paddy hoped they would, if he waited long enough.

The wait was boring, however, and Paddy soon decided to find some more amusing way to make people sorry. He turned from the window and couldn't miss seeing the thing that glowed on top of the wardrobe.

It was a weird thing, with a dusty head and flat rolling eyes. Its stick legs dangled over the edge of the wardrobe, and its feet wore high-laced boots. Its arms were painfully thin, dragged down by the weight of outsized hands. The green glow that showed it up in the dark room gave it no beauty. Paddy-last had never seen anything so ugly and wretched.

The thing didn't frighten Paddy, because he knew that Aengus was in the next room, and the rest of the family were just down the stairs, probably making cocoa for supper. Besides, Paddy thought he knew what the thing was: a night-noise, one of those things that rustles around, making people lie awake wondering, 'What's that noise?'

'What are you doing here?' he asked it. 'Nobody sleeps here, not until tomorrow night, and anyhow, you're not supposed to creep about until we're all in bed.'

The thing gargled and seemed to say 'Pocket'. Its voice rattled horribly.

What would a night-noise say 'pocket' for? Perhaps it meant 'packet' or 'peck it'. Paddy-last decided 'packet' made the most sense.

'Huh,' he said, 'bad enough that you keep me awake, wondering if you're monsters or burglars. Now you want presents as well.'

'Pocket,' the thing muttered sadly.

'If you are saying "pocket",' Paddy-last said, 'why didn't you pocket the Historic Doorknob before we started fighting over it, and I had to throw it out the window? It's unlucky enough, it would suit you. And Robbie figures it's secretly magic, and something's going to come looking for it someday, but he was only trying to scare me. Like you do,' he added resentfully.

The creature shuffled about, boots hollowly knocking against the wardrobe door. Paddy looked at it with dislike: it was such a miserable tatter of a thing, to have made all the spooky noises that scared him at night.

When the thing sat still again, it began a long hoarse speech, crackling and whistling, impossible to understand. There was a faint suggestion of music in the racket, which interested Paddy. He was always making up songs, himself, and could recognize music in the unlikeliest noises.

But after listening awhile, the faint music became a whine, and still Paddy couldn't guess what it was trying to say.

'I don't know what you have to complain about,' he interrupted. 'You get to lie about all day, planning how to worry people that want to sleep, people that have enough problems, like me.

'How would you like to have big brothers and a sister that drag you all over the countryside, looking for an adventure you don't want? Or, what if you had a baby cousin coming to mess up your holidays? And you don't have to get up early tomorrow, to tidy for visitors.

'No, you just creep out at night, and rustle the curtains, or creak the stairs, or groan a door. And shut up when I'm talking to you,' he said, as the thing sighed as though to speak. 'You've made enough noise, every night of my life. About time I got to noise back at you.'

The thing made sorry sounds, its dusty head bobbing. Paddy knew it could never scare him again. He even felt rather sorry for it, and ready to console its wretchedness.

'Okay,' he said, moving towards the door. 'At least you're sorry. Anyhow, I don't care about their old adventure, because *they* didn't find anything, but *I* found an old mug handle and a plastic flower and an ancient comb, and I'm going to try wishing on them. In stories, it's always the weirdest things that grant wishes.'

The creature's glow suddenly brightened to an excited green, and its fresh burst of babble gave Paddy pause. He stood with his hand on the doorknob, fascinated by the thing's pathetic urgency. What could it be saying? Should he fetch his brother Aengus to translate? Aengus fancied himself a Great Explorer, and Great Explorers had to understand outlandish languages. Or would Lizzie know better, she being so friendly to wild animals? Perhaps Robbie would know the most, since he was the eldest.

But Paddy wasn't ready to approach his brothers or sister. They might still be angry over the Historic Doorknob. Besides, he could imagine what they would say, if he asked them to translate a green-glowing night-noise in the spare room.

Meanwhile, the creature garbled on and on, waving its awkward hands and nodding its dusty head. The word 'pocket' came through the cracks in its voice, and perhaps the word 'wishes'.

'You want to make a wish?'

The thing, still gabbling, jumped off the wardrobe. It

4

floated eerily towards him, clumsy boots skimming the floor. That was a bit too much for Paddy-last: he escaped onto the bright landing and closed the door firmly behind him.

He ran to his brothers' room, and was glad to find Aengus there, poring over the latest map.

'What do you want?' Aengus looked up from the map which he had spread on the floor. 'Get out, this is our room.' He smoothed the precious chart, to warn Paddy's trespassing feet away.

Paddy-last dithered and said, 'There's a night-noise in the spare room.'

'So? You won't be sleeping there. Go away.'

'But it's trying to talk,' Paddy said hopelessly. 'I couldn't understand it, and it came after me.'

Aengus sat back on his heels. 'Can you understand me?' he asked.

'Yes,' Paddy squeaked.

'Then: get lost, or I'll come after you.'

Aengus resumed studying his masterpiece map, and Paddy-last wandered down the stairs. He went to the kitchen where cheerful, plain noises soon cancelled the green glow's grumbles. Paddy-last involved himself in cocoa and biscuits, without wasting any more worry on that feeble night-noise.

CHAPTER 2

By the Dawn's Early Light

If dawn really did crack, no one in the country would hear it for the daily chorusing of the early birds. They begin with a timid whistle or two, a questioning call, and from there work up a riot of sound as loud as any of the city traffic the four children had once slept through, on city mornings in the past.

This fateful morning, Lizzie and Paddy-last slumbered on, undisturbed by the winged uproar, and so would have Aengus and Robbie but for the alarm. The bullying ring screamed at five o'clock exactly. Aengus staggered out to choke it off, and was collared by Robbie on his way back to bed.

The room was still in darkness. Outside, there was a hint of silver on the night.

Robbie said, 'I've been meaning to see a sunrise ever since we moved into this room.'

He propped Aengus against the window sill and threw up the sash of the east window. At once, a cool breeze billowed into the room, laden with the scents of the sun.

'You want to see real unexplored territory,' he whispered excitedly, 'you just watch this.'

'I'm watching,' Aengus shivered.

The sun rose in glowing banks on a silver lagoon. The

brothers hung out of the window, convinced that the tumbling, fiery shores and the still, flaming waters were as real as the grey-green countryside below. Aengus chewed his knuckles, trying to figure how he might reach that land, while Robbie imagined all that he would do and see there. They were unconscious of passing time, and of the rising birdsong, until the sun broke through at last. Then the glowing banks and white waters shredded into long pink banners across the sky. The boys transferred their hopes to nearer territory.

By this, the dawn chorus was deafening. In the rocky field beyond the garden hedges, That-Cat primly stalked the singers. Her brownish coat blended with the background.

'Missed!' Robbie crowed, as That-Cat pounced, and wings flew upwards.

That-Cat heard, but didn't look. She sat down to wash, pretending she had meant to miss.

'It's all over,' Aengus sighed. 'Now, let's get the tidying done. I'll wake Lizzie. I'll really wake her: it was her idea to get up at the crack of dawn, instead of tidying last night.'

'What's the hurry?' Robbie asked. 'Wait awhile. That-Cat might try again, and we can foil her feline schemes.'

Aengus reminded him, 'They're coming after breakfast. Uncle Conor's not like Daddy. He's always on time.'

'Aunt Ina never is. She might delay him. Look: there's the blackbird Lizzie was trying to track down. I wonder what she'd give, to find its nest?'

'Won't take us a second,' Aengus insisted. 'We can just shove everything into the cupboards, or under the bed. They won't know the difference.'

'Peter will drag it all out into the guilty light of day,' Robbie said. 'Imagine, tidying for people to dump a baby into the midst of. And then they'll buzz off on their holiday, leaving all wreckage and Peter behind. I wish we had found that adventure we were searching for. Now all our summer memories will be Peter.'

'Peter's okay,' Aengus said. He yawned. 'He'll be a comrade in arms, a natural phenomenon. Sunrises are natural phenomena.'

'So are earthquakes,' said Robbie, 'volcanoes, and man-eating tigers. Natural phenomenon! You can talk scientifically until you're blue-moulded, Aengus, but you will never change a baby's phenomenal nature, or my mind. Look at all the trouble he's caused, and he isn't even here yet. Why did we get nagged and slagged all week long, until we swore to get up at the crack of dawn? Because our rooms are a mess. And why a mess? Because you and I had to move into this room. And why was that? Because of the natural phenomenon. Wake up when I'm talking to you, Aengus.'

'I'm awake,' said Aengus, straightening and knocking his head on the window frame.

'We should even blame last night on your phenomenon,' Robbie continued. 'If we hadn't had to divide everything, on account of moving rooms, Paddy-last wouldn't have tried to pretend the Historic Doorknob was his, or have to throw it through the window when we proved it wasn't. Look! Look! Look!' he interrupted himself to point out That-Cat, successfully pouncing. 'The beast, the creeper, she's caught something. Next, she'll come howling starvedly at the kitchen door. How is it she can fool Mammy and we can't?'

'Come on, Robbie,' Aengus said. He turned away from the window.

Robbie mused, 'And they talk about brute intelligence, as though it weren't worth having. Maybe it's an instinct cats need to survive.'

'Robbie,' Aengus said hoarsely.

Robbie looked at his brother. 'Wow! You look green,' he said with interest. 'That must be the dawn light. Do I look green?'

'I wonder am I asleep. Am I asleep?' Aengus asked. 'Or maybe it's because we haven't had breakfast yet.'

'What are you raving about?' Robbie wondered.

'Well, look, don't you see what I don't see?'

Robbie frowned. It wasn't like Aengus to talk such rubbish. He turned into the room.

The bedroom was bright now, brilliantly so. The sun not only lightened, but lingered: in the deep gloss of the carpet, in the high polish of the furniture, in the clear glitter of the window panes. Every nook, cranny, and corner made space for some sort of shine or sparkle; every item within the four walls found some excuse to twinkle. Only Robbie's sword, made from a lightning-struck tree and hanging on the wall over his bed, was dull and untouched. But that was barely noticeable among the dancing sparkles.

'What—' Robbie began, staring between the points of light. He took a second and a third look, but no amount of looks could see what wasn't there. No *Victory* model with spars, rigging, and glue littered the floor; the map of local history with its pencils, rulers, rubbers and pencil-toppers was gone. No papers bulged from the presses, no clothes lay draped over the chairs.

After perhaps the tenth useless glance, Robbie bounded across the gleaming carpet to open drawers and cupboards. One look within was enough to show that more was missing than met the eye.

'The sneaks,' he seethed. 'The creeping do-gooders.'

'Who?' Aengus weakly asked, utterly stricken by the loss of his map.

'Lizard and Padders,' said Robbie. 'Just because we had the alarm, and they had to wake up alone. Wait until I get my hands on them.' He ran out of the room.

Feebly, Aengus followed.

In the room across the landing, Paddy-last curled up in a ball and rolled to the floor, howling. Lizzie shrieked, swinging a beanbag frog. Ducking the frog in vain, Robbie shouted accusations and insults, and took up the furry snake to defend himself. Aengus sank greenly onto an empty chair.

Their mother appeared like magic, surprising everyone but Aengus, who couldn't be surprised by what this mad morning would dream up next. She grabbed the frog and the snake, and stumbled over Paddy while skilfully delivering a lecture at the same time.

'I knew it,' she concluded her speech triumphantly, 'I knew you couldn't be trusted to do anything without a row!'

Robbie and Lizzie tried to set her straight, but of course she wouldn't listen to reason.

'I don't want to hear it,' she said. 'Be quiet, Paddy, no one's touching you. And look at Aengus, he's fainting away. I suppose you couldn't be bothered with anything so sensible as breakfast, though I've told you a thousand times—' and she hustled the green explorer away, still talking.

As soon as she was out of the room, Robbie turned on Lizzie once more, letting her know in a clear manner what he thought of people who thieved and stole and vandalized. Lizzie, however, ignored him. She was staring beyond, her scowl fading as her jaw fell. Robbie's words trickled away as she scrambled off the bed, fell over Paddy-last, and began to eagerly search the wardrobe, the drawers, and under the furniture for all those things she couldn't see. She even looked up the chimney, which Robbie hadn't thought of doing.

Watching her, Robbie felt an awful sinking sensation, as sickly green as Aengus.

'It was Paddy-last,' Lizzie panted, crouched by the empty orchestra pit, commonly known as a fireplace. 'He wished last night. Even the spider is gone.'

'The little idiot,' Robbie gulped.

'Now don't start all over,' said his returning mother. 'It really is too bad you had to finish such splendid work with a quarrel. I'm sure I've never seen two rooms look so clean, nor heard you begin your capers so early. Six o'clock!' She tugged at the lumpish Paddy-last. 'Now go back to bed, and we'll forget all about it.'

Lizzie and Robbie cringed at the thought of waiting any longer in the gleaming disaster area.

'Can't we go for a walk instead?' Robbie pleaded. 'Only to the fields. I couldn't sleep. I'm too awake.'

'Please,' Lizzie also begged. 'We'll breakfast first. Please, please, please.' She hopped with each 'please' to underline her earnestness.

'Well,' said their mother, considering the truly

beautiful tidiness. 'I suppose so. But go quietly and dress warmly and be sure you do eat something.'

'We will, we will,' they eagerly promised, willing to sacrifice anything that the tidiness had left, in order to get away.

Lizzie pummelled Paddy-last into his clothes. She chased him down to the kitchen, before he could take in the emptiness of his orchestra pit. They boiled the kettle and burned the toast for Robbie and Aengus. Robbie had a hard time, getting Aengus up and out. Aengus had begun a dream about lost tribes, and he was reluctant to go back to the nightmare about lost maps. He only agreed to get up at last, with the promise of getting right out of the desolate house.

The breakfast was gulped, and the four children were out of the front gate before swallowing half.

'Looks the same as usual,' Lizzie noted, stopping to inspect the house from outside.

'Come on,' Robbie urged. 'Something might be watching from the windows.'

Lizzie hastily came on, shuddering.

'Why are we out?' asked Paddy-last. He was only now waking up. 'We're supposed to be committing tidiness for Uncle Conor and Aunt Ina.'

'It's committed,' Robbie said. Then he bit his tongue, wondering how to break the news that the orchestra was gone, and the orchestra pit was a mere fireplace once more. Paddy would insist on returning and searching. Robbie didn't want to return: apart from the creepy cleanliness, this would be their only chance to take council. The visitors were due before lunch, and all hope of council would be gone.

'I never saw anything like it,' said Aengus, too full of vanished maps to consider orchestras. 'What happened? Were you really wishing, Paddy? If your wishes came true, after all our search for adventure, all our room-moving, and toil and tribulations, that you sneaked out of besides breaking a window with the Historic Doorknob—' Aengus paused to take a deep and almost sobbing breath. 'Well, then,' he finished, 'now I know what poet's justice is.'

'I'm not a poet,' Paddy-last said. 'And anyhow, it wasn't my fault. Everybody knows that Historic Doorknob's jinxed.'

'Why did you want it, then?' Lizzie asked. 'We told you it was an heirloom.'

'Oh, skip that stupid doorknob,' Robbie said. 'We don't need that, to have problems.'

'But maybe that's it!' Aengus shouted. 'Maybe the tidiness is the Historic Doorknob's revenge.'

'Cop on,' Robbie suggested. 'We've had that doorknob in the family for generations.'

They came to the fields by the peat bog without further discussion. An icy black water ran between the flat russet land and the slightly drier fields. Over this stream, a cement bridge led to the path trailing away into wet distances. The children stopped on the bridge, seating themselves on the rough parapet with feet dangling over the water. Their arrival startled a heron fishing there. It flapped awkwardly away, legs dragging the air.

Lizzie finished her apple and threw the core as far as she could without falling off the bridge. Then she said, 'Maybe it wasn't magic at all, but something natural.

Like burglars. They're famous for clean sweeps, aren't they?'

'They are not,' Robbie said impatiently. 'The navy invented clean sweeps. And besides, I don't see why even the most poverty-stricken burglar in the world would sneak off with your mouldy old bones, or Paddy's junk, or my wrecked ship, or Aengus's maps. Besides the spider and all the rest.'

'Might have been a scientific burglar,' Lizzie said without conviction. 'Anyhow, my bones aren't mouldy. They get thoroughly cleaned inside the owl, and when he spits them out, they're neatly wrapped.'

'It wasn't burglars,' Robbie said stubbornly.

Paddy-last asked, 'What wasn't burglars?'

Robbie let his apple core fall into the water. He stared down at the rippling rings, wondering. Could this really be magic, at last? Robbie had read enough to know that magic can be awkward and contrary, that wishes are never as simple as the words that express them. And this tidiness was entirely awkward and contrary.

'Still,' Lizzie was insisting, 'there could be a perfectly natural reason. There's stranger things in nature.'

'It's not a natural tidiness,' said Aengus. 'And tidiness isn't natural anyhow. Especially phenomenal tidiness.'

Lizzie ignored him, for she was the nature expert of the family. 'Birds migrating,' she said, 'and lemmings, and magpies. Why, maybe it was magpies! Mr Thompson says they're extra plentiful this year, on account of the soft winter, and a magpie stole a five-pound note of his once.'

She rambled on, giving examples of magpie theft and other interesting information. Only Paddy-last listened, half-asleep and still wondering why he'd been dragged out of bed, if there was no tidying to be done. Robbie and Aengus got down to considering what adventure might be had from a magic tidiness. Aengus found the problem difficult, as his mind kept returning to the disaster of his lost maps, particularly his latest map of local lost civilizations, which young Mr MacAdam had been helping him draw up. Robbie's only difficulty was making up his mind about the magic tidier: hero or villain? A hero couldn't be guilty of such desolation, but then, who wanted a villain sneaking around their own house? Their parents wouldn't like it.

'Anyhow,' Robbie broke in on Lizzie to say, 'we have to get rid of it. And be sure you don't make any wishes until we do.'

For a moment they didn't know what he was talking about. Then, 'So you think it is some magic,' said Lizzie. 'Well, I don't see why we should get rid of it, if you're right. There's lots we could wish for.'

'That's what people say, when they know their wishes aren't going to come true,' Robbie said. 'For one thing, nothing is for nothing, not even in magic. We'd get the bill sometime. And then, what about other people wishing? Like what if Paddy-last wished he was bigger than us, or you wished for a wild animal friend, and it ate one of us, or what if Mammy wished we wouldn't row? Do you want to be struck dumb? And besides, how would we explain the loot to the parents? They wouldn't believe us, they'd think we were liars and robbers. And I could tell you lots more reasons, but it all comes to the same thing: we can't have a magic in the house that is granting wishes right, left, and centre.'

'That's right,' said Aengus. 'Wishing's no fun, anyhow. Where would all the Great Adventures be, if Great Explorers just wished they were there and back?'

'Where?' asked Paddy-last. He couldn't follow the discussion at all, and hoped to get some part clear.

'No where,' said Robbie. 'Like my model fleet, Aengus's maps, Lizzie's museum, and your orchestra.'

'What do you mean?' Paddy-last turned pale.

'You wished them all away,' Lizzie said. 'Wishing for tidiness on that junk you found, you wished everything away. How could magic know your stupid orchestra wasn't rubbish? We could hardly tell, ourselves.'

'Do you mean,' Paddy asked, wanting to get this quite clear, 'that the mug handle, the plastic flower, and the old comb I found and wished on, are magic after all, just like in books when people find rings and things all accidentally?'

'No,' Lizzie said. 'All that junk you wished on is gone, too. It was only rubbish, and the real magic got rid of it.'

'Small loss,' Aengus said.

'But my orchestra wasn't rubbish,' Paddy-last said. 'It was tidy, in its own orchestra pit.'

'Sure,' Robbie said. He could see that both Aengus and Lizzie wanted to ask: if bits of tyre tube, boxes of lentils, and pieces of cardboard weren't rubbish, what was? But Paddy, like them all, had suffered enough in losing, without adding insult. Robbie continued, 'Now, let's think about how to find this magic curse and get rid of it. We have to figure it out now, because once we're stuck with the infant cousin, we'll be at our wits' ends. So start thinking, and don't say anything unless it's a good idea.'

They shut up. Paddy-last was speechless, anyhow, as the realization sank in.

In the thoughtful stillness, the heron was encouraged to return, so huge as to be almost terrifying. A watchful stoat's curiosity was aroused, and it ducked snakily along for a closer, beady-eyed look. The children might have sat thinking forever, fascinating the stoat, but the countryside was awakening now. Doors slammed and motors revved, sending flat echoes across the meadows to the bog. A barking of dogs in turn marked the progress of the bread van. And a dull plodding finally sent the heron flapping away and the stoat under cover.

'You're up early,' Badger Joyce shouted from behind his cows. 'Open the gate, will ye?'

They jumped to obey, shaking off all their wondering stillness for the ordinary work of cows. The gate was a real struggle, and required full attention, for it wasn't really a gate at all, but an arrangement of branches, wire, and twine.

Lizzie said, 'You know you'll have to manage without us from now on, on account of Peter.' For the children usually helped Badger in bringing the cows home in the evenings.

'I'll get a dog,' said Badger, driving his herd through the open gate. 'A good dog is worth ten men,' he said, 'and about four kids.' He hurried a straggler with his stick and began rearranging the branches. 'A proper gate,' he said, admiring his work. 'No one forgets to close a gate like this.'

'You should get one for your front garden, then,' said Aengus. 'Miss Joyce wouldn't be blaming us for leaving it open.'

'The postman wouldn't like it,' said Badger. 'Besides, Ned Graham is collecting a new gate for us in town. That old one is bewitched: there's no pleasing it.'

'Like our Historic Doorknob,' said Paddy-last.

The pasture gate closed, they all headed for home together, the children falling in on either side of Badger. As they went, Lizzie asked,

'Did Mr Thompson ever tell you about a magpie that took a five-pound note of his, once?'

'He did,' Badger said. 'A four-legged magpie that came in last for the hurdle.'

'A race horse,' guessed Robbie.

'That's her. At least, they called her a racer.'

'Oh,' said brothers and sister together.

'So what would you call it,' Lizzie asked, 'if you found everything suddenly tidy and everything gone? I don't mean ordinary neat, but super-super tidy.'

'That's those pesky fairies,' Badger promptly replied. 'They're awful tricksters.'

'We don't believe in fairies,' Paddy-last said coldly.

'I'm sure they're worried,' said Badger, not at all offended. 'They're a wicked crew, always up to mischief, whether you believe in them or not. There are those as can make them fetch and carry, like old Mrs White, rest her, but then, she was a Madden.'

'What,' asked Aengus, 'has being a Madden got to do with it?'

'Nothing, now,' said Badger. 'She was the last of them. Good morning!' he suddenly bellowed.

A distant Mr Regan waved.

Robbie seized the chance to ask, 'Are you going to buy his red heifer?' for cows are not a joking matter. Of all things, Robbie hated being teased with fairies.

When they reached home, the children were grabbed by their parents and nagged into good clothes and a proper breakfast. Paddy-last resisted, at first refusing to go upstairs and see that his orchestra really was gone, and then refusing to come down, in hopes of finding the orchestra had been safely tidied into a cupboard. Then he wanted to wish it all back, but Lizzie swore she'd burn it, if he even thought the wish. She had Robbie and Aengus's support, and Paddy was forced to surrender.

'But I don't see why not,' he sobbed reasonably. 'You could wish too.'

'I don't want anything from a magic rubbish dump, no thanks,' said Lizzie. 'Magic rats have probably chewed everything to bits, anyhow. Remember what happened in that story, "The Monkey's Paw".'

'Nothing happened,' argued Paddy, all in vain.

They sat down to the proper breakfast without a proper appetite. Their parents made it worse by forever praising the dreadful deed of tidiness. Perhaps they thought to encourage their children to be tidy always, but they soon gave up that hope. Robbie made them change the subject by scraping a butter knife into the jam jar. Aengus added a wet spoon to the sugar, Lizzie knocked over the milk jug, and Paddy-last hid his crusts on the floor under the table. He didn't know That-Cat had gone out a moment before, though he ought to have known she was never around when wanted.

As Robbie had foretold, there was no further chance to take council. The visitors arrived shortly after breakfast. The children met them in the front garden, where Aunt Ina showered them with gifts: HMS *Shannon* for Robbie, a fat atlas for Aengus, an official Nature Journal for Lizzie, and for Paddy-last, a xylophone. Then she undid all the good work, by giving them Peter to mind while she and Uncle Conor politely visited in the house.

Robbie had an idea that Peter could be left loose while they got down to dealing with the magic menace. He soon learned his mistake. Peter was just a year old, quite an ordinary baby, fond of eating strange things, of hitting people, of rooting in the ground.

Robbie began with, 'I think we should test the wishes with something harmless. Would you ever take that beetle away from him, Lizzie?'

Beetle removed, howls threatened, and Aengus hastily offered a dusty square of chocolate in its place. Aengus was always hoarding sweets, to the annoyance of his brothers and sister.

'Right,' said Robbie, seeing Peter gnaw contentedly and messily. 'Test the wishes. Maybe we'll be able to see where the power comes from. You're not listening.'

'I am,' said Aengus.

Lizzie and Paddy-last weren't. They were sadly watching the infant cousin do everything with the chocolate but eat it. The waste nearly broke their hearts. Robbie called them to order with thumps, and repeated all he had said.

'You'll be wasting your time,' Lizzie declared. 'There

aren't harmless wishes, not if Badger's right about pesky fairies.'

'No such thing,' Paddy-last sneered.

'I don't mean those kind,' said Lizzie. 'I mean the kind Badger means. After all, he doesn't read anything but the *Farmers' Journal* and stuff about country music.'

Robbie asked scornfully, 'So what kind of fairies do you get from the *Farmers' Journal* and country music?'

'Secret magic people,' said Lizzie, 'that have secret lives in folklore, with banshees and ancient curses. They're not fairies, they're, well—'

'Lost civilizations,' Aengus eagerly supplied.

'Could there be hiding civilizations,' Paddy asked doubtfully, thinking of the thing in the spare room. 'Could one of them stray out into open day and not find its way back and shelter in our house?'

'Watch out!' everyone shouted, drowning the question.

'Owwerr!' said Paddy-last at the same time.

The chocolate-coated baby had crept away and had found the cow-driving sticks that had been carefully hidden under the hedge. He brandished them triumphantly, delighted with Paddy's response.

'I knew it would be like this,' Robbie said. He scrambled a safe distance away. 'Someone disarm the little brute before he commits a mortal wound.'

'He'll howl,' Lizzie shrewdly predicted.

'Let him,' said Paddy-last.

Aengus sighed deeply. 'You're great adventurers all right, scared of a little natural phenomenon. Wait.' He ran into the house, and shortly returned with a rubber frog that lived in the bathroom. He squeaked the frog, tantalizingly, in Peter's face. Peter laughed, let fall the sticks, and took the frog in both hands. Lizzie sneaked the sticks away.

'Will we make the wishes now?' Aengus said. 'All the grown-ups are jawing in the sittingroom. I'll mind Peter.'

'Mind you do,' said Robbie.

So he led them indoors and upstairs, Aengus carrying the comrade in arms.

'We'll try the landing first,' Robbie said. 'What will we wish?'

Lizzie said, 'I wish we had some chocolate.'

And they had. Chocolate rattled out of nowhere in bars, boxes, and bags. There was every kind, as Lizzie hadn't said what kind. There was any amount, as Lizzie hadn't said what amount. It covered the landing floor and began sliding down the stairs.

Except for Peter, who thought it all great fun, the children were stunned. In their heart of hearts, not one of them had believed that a wish could be granted like this. The morning's desolation had angered, but this was frightening. Here was evidence of a stow-away power right in their own house. No place was safe. Moreover, here was evidence which would get them into terrible trouble, if any grown-ups chose this moment to come upstairs.

Lizzie gathered her wits first. She got down on hands and knees, and began to scrape together the awful reward.

'Help me,' she said to her stupified brothers.

They unstuck themselves. Aengus parked Peter in the linen closet, and Robbie fetched large plastic bags from the kitchen. It was easily the worst thing that had ever happened, far more dangerous than any amount of broken windows, rows, or tidinesses. Each time a grown-up moved downstairs, the children froze, and still the chocolate kept pouring down. Peter howled in the linen closet, until Aengus threw in a block of chocolate. That-Cat came up and played and pounced. Paddy-last chased her and caged her in a bedroom. She yowled and Peter was inspired to howl again.

'It's got to stop,' Robbie panted. 'I wish it would.'

And it did: the chocolate, the cat, and the infant.

For a brief moment, the children sat exhausted among the loot, revelling in the silence. Then it occurred to Aengus to check just how the magic had managed to silence Peter. He opened the linen closet, and the children got the biggest fright of all. They shouted together. Peter started and yet again began to cry. As for the weird and ugly creature that had been entertaining him, it gargled and vanished.

'It's the night-noise!' Paddy recognized. 'The one from the spare room! Go after it!'

But at that moment, the children were called and had to spend the rest of the day amusing their uncle and aunt. They made many attempts at escape, but the harder they tried, the more their parents suspected them of being up to no good.

'No adventurers,' Robbie said, when bedtime came without success, 'however tortured and eaten by cannibals or wild animals, can ever have suffered like we have today. First thing tomorrow!'

With that hope, they could go to bed in peace.

CHAPTER 3

Wishing for More Trouble

'What are you doing?' Aengus whispered into the softly rustling darkness.

'What does it look like?' Having dressed, Robbie felt about in the dark for his running shoes.

'Looks like the middle of the night,' said Aengus.

Robbie said, 'Well, it's not.' He found his shoes and put them on.

A little while before, Robbie had wakened with the sort of feeling he used to get, when remembering too late some school lesson he had forgotten to learn. For a moment, he hadn't been able to figure out why he should feel like that, during holidays. Then, hearing a door close, he remembered: the Historic Doorknob. If he couldn't get at the secret magic person, he knew exactly where to find the Historic Doorknob.

'Since you're awake,' he told Aengus now, 'get up and let me have your sheets.'

'Not a fire escape!' Aengus was horrified. 'Not now! You can't, Robbie. You know how Mammy and Daddy get all upset, if we do anything while there's visitors in the house.'

'Sure,' Robbie said, unmoved. 'That's because they're afraid the visitors will go around, telling everyone how wild we are. But these visitors aren't going to find out,

24

because Mammy and Daddy aren't going to know. Get up, Aengus, or I'll pull the sheets from under you.'

Aengus got up. There was no point in reminding Robbie how their first, and last, fire escape had landed them in the frying pan. Robbie would only reply that there was no Maire Graham around, this time, to mistake them for burglars, and ring the police.

'Got a torch?' Robbie asked next, as he tied the fire escape to the radiator below the window.

'I don't know,' Aengus said confusedly. 'I think it's tidied away somewhere. Uncle Fergus says it's easier to see in the dark without one.' Uncle Fergus was their oldest and wisest uncle.

'He just doesn't like us using up his batteries,' said Robbie. 'Anyhow, the moon's coming up, so I guess I'll see as much as I have to.'

'But what are you doing?' Aengus wondered. 'You said we'd start the search for the magic person in the morning.'

Robbie climbed through the window. 'That's different. I'm going after the Historic Doorknob,' he said just before vanishing.

After a surprised moment, Aengus rushed to the window to ask, 'Why?' But he was too late. Leaning over the sill, Aengus saw his brother, a vague lumpish shadow, swing off the greyly glowing fire escape, to merge with the blacks and whites of the garden below. Looking for a doorknob like that, Aengus reflected, Robbie was looking for trouble. And anyhow, why?

A hissed, 'What's up?' made Aengus bang his head on the sash. He turned furiously on Lizzie, a pale figure with a grey face and a length of pink nightgown shining whitely in the darkness.

'You might have knocked,' he said. 'Robbie's out looking for the Historic Doorknob.'

'Oh, good,' Lizzie sighed with relief. 'I couldn't sleep, when I remembered it. I hope it's still there. And besides, Peter was growling. He must be dreaming he's a tiger or something,' she said enviously.

'Maybe,' said Aengus, not interested in natural phenomena at the moment. 'Why did the doorknob keep you awake?'

'Lots of reasons,' Lizzie said. She crowded in beside him, to hang out of the window. 'What caused a row the last night, just when we were getting agreeable? What broke a window? And remember when Robbie told Paddy that it was secretly magic and someone would come for it someday?'

'He was just putting Paddy off. We've had that doorknob for years. Even Robbie said so, this morning.'

'Well, think of the kind of magic we have here, and the kind of doorknob it is, and then wonder what brought the magic here, of all places.'

Aengus thought: the doorknob wasn't called Historic for nothing. It had got stuck in mouths, come off in hands, and had caused rows for generations. But it had never got lost, nor worn away with time, as had other, nicer heirlooms.

Lizzie continued, 'I think that maybe our magic secret person came here on a quest, looking for the Historic Doorknob, or maybe something about the doorknob drew the magic secret person here, as it wandered lost, an outcast and folorn creature without a friend. Must be an unlucky outcast, too, to meet Paddy first, and not one of us. Paddy wouldn't befriend a night-noise. It will be glad of my friendship, won't it? If we hadn't been tied up with Peter, I could have been its firm friend by now.'

Aengus said, 'Huh. But if you're right about the magic person being lost, it will be gladder of a map-maker and a navigator, than any amount of useless friends.'

'It will be glad of both,' Lizzie generously allowed.

They stared down at Robbie. It was impossible to tell what he was doing, except that he was doing it very slowly.

'Poor creature,' Lizzie murmured. 'What a fright we gave it, when we all shouted this afternoon.'

'What a fright it gave us,' said Aengus. 'And what a lot of chocolate. We're going to have to shift it, you know, that chocolate. When Mammy was bringing Aunt Ina around the house, she was bragging about our tidiness, and saying we even cleaned under the beds. Only for Robbie saying he wouldn't bet on it, Mammy would have made herself a liar.'

'I don't care about the chocolate,' Lizzie said. 'I want to find our secret friend, and help it.'

'Hmm,' said Aengus. He looked out over the black mass of the woods, to the starry bears of the sky, and wondered how they would manage an adventure in the house. Their parents would object, and Aengus wasn't keen on the idea, himself. Home was a refuge when adventures got tough, or it was supposed to be.

'Tomorrow,' he said, 'as soon as Uncle Conor and Aunt Ina take off, I'm going down to young Mr MacAdam and starting a new map. We're going to need it.'

Lizzie didn't reply. She was soaking in the light of the waxing moon, the late hour, the furtive noises of darkness. This was the proper setting for adventure, and not a house noisy with happy visitors. 'I wish,' she said, 'we could be sure our magic secret person is okay.'

She got her wish at once, although for a good while she didn't recognize it. The secret magic person sent its 'all's well' by button box. The box came battering the door open and rattling through the air. It landed on a chair where it waited a moment before rolling off. The buttons scattered, as the tin box flew open. The box itself rolled on, to fetch up against the far wall. The din of crashing drums and clashing cymbals would have made Paddy-last sick with envy.

A deep and listening hush followed, and then the creak of investigating footsteps.

'Quick,' Aengus shoved Lizzie. 'Get into Robbie's bed and cover up.'

Lizzie dived across the room, wincing as the buttons gouged her bare feet. Aengus began at once to undo the fire escape. His father would forgive anything but that.

Despite his best efforts, the light went on before the first hitch was loosened. Aengus sprang to his feet, hoping to hide the evidence behind his back. The sudden light made him blink, but he could see enough to recognize his father standing in the doorway.

'What are you doing?'

Aengus opened his mouth to answer 'nothing' but the word wheezed flat. He could see quite well, now, and what he saw were Robbie's pyjamas huddled on the floor.

'You used to be a lot quicker,' said his father, having waited in vain for an excuse. 'What are you hiding, glueing yourself to the wall like that?' He approached.

Aengus flinched nimbly out of reach, his mind racing. The fire escape didn't matter now, the important thing was to keep Lizzie and Robbie out of it. For some reason known only to parents, their mother and father could forgive and forget solitary criminals more easily than they could a conspiracy.

So while his father's back was turned to haul in the fire escape, Aengus mouthed a desperate wish. The pyjamas vanished with an instant uncanniness that unnerved him.

'Well?' said his father, making Aengus jump. 'Have you thought up an excuse yet?'

'I knocked the box over,' Aengus stammered feebly, gesturing to the scatter of buttons.

'I guessed that,' said his father. 'Now go back to the beginning of the story.' He bundled the fire escape under his arm.

'I wasn't going down, honest,' Aengus said. 'I was only going to pull it in, in case a burglar came up and robbed us. I promise!'

'You'd better go to bed,' said his father, 'and see whether you can't dream up something better than that.'

'Okay,' Aengus agreed readily. 'What about the, I mean, the sheets?' he added, seeing his father was heading for the door with the bundle still under his arm.

'I wouldn't trust you with a tea towel,' said his father, unkindly. 'Get into bed. I'll turn out the light.'

29

So Aengus got, burrowing down beneath the blankets. He didn't breathe until the light went off, and the footsteps had gone well away.

'Figures,' murmured Lizzie.

'Be quiet,' Aengus furiously hissed. He would have liked to add a few remarks on her rash wish, but knew his father would be listening for voices. Wrenching his mind away from the worry of dreaming up an excuse for the morning, Aengus concentrated on the problem of Robbie.

Lizzie wasn't prepared to wait long in the scratchy sheetless bed. She counted sixty, five times, and sat up.

'Now what?' she whispered.

'He took the fire escape,' Aengus said. 'If I could have thrown it out, we'd have got it up again with a bit of string. But no, he had to go and confiscate it.'

'I don't suppose we have string, anyhow,' said Lizzie. She stared into the darkness, thinking hard. But she couldn't think, not in this room with night noises so different from those in her own room, and not in this bed of prickly blankets and no sheets. What was that creak behind her? What ticked in the corner? What rustled in the chimney? And what had Robbie stored in his pillow, which was now sticking into her back?

'Come on,' she said, getting out of the bed, unable to lie in it any longer. 'We have to get him in before he does something desperate. Do you think I could sneak down to the kitchen and let him in?'

'You couldn't sneak a button box by magic,' Aengus sneered, glad of the chance to say so.

Lizzie said, 'I guess the secret magic person was

trying to say it felt as bright as a button. How about sliding down the bannister?'

'And up it?'

'Get up, anyhow,' she said, prodding him. 'Lying there won't get him in, and he'll know a story you can tell Daddy in the morning.'

Aengus swung out of bed, and they went together to the window. There was no sign of Robbie in the strangely shadowed garden. He must have hidden when the light went on.

'Doesn't look like our own back garden, does it?' Lizzie whispered.

'No, it doesn't,' Aengus agreed. 'It looks secret and sinister.'

'Why, of course!' Lizzie exclaimed. 'We can wish. Not for the fire escape, Daddy might notice, but for something. A ladder?'

'No way, not after your message. What we need is something quiet and easily concealed.'

'A rope ladder?'

'A clothes line. I wish we had a clothes line.'

Immediately, something bulky flopped about their feet. Lizzie squeaked, startled, and then felt about.

'Now you've done it,' she said. 'A clothes line, and with clothes on it.'

'Never mind that.' Aengus snatched at the cold, damp pile. 'Let's get them off.'

They set to, pulling the clothes off the line. Pegs snapped and flew in the darkness. Occasionally, something ripped. There seemed no end to the line.

'Must belong to the army,' Aengus muttered.

Lizzie stuffed the clothes under Robbie's bed beside

the chocolate. She tried to find the pegs to hide as well, but that was impossible in the dark.

'Forget them,' Aengus said. 'Let's get Robbie in first.'

He tied the now empty line to the radiator pipes. He threw the line out, and flapped it against the house to attract Robbie's attention.

'Where is he?' Lizzie worried, when he didn't appear.

'Here he comes,' said Aengus, seeing one shadow detach itself from the rest.

They had never seen Robbie climb so fast, flying up without seeming to put a hand to the rope at all. His haste made them suspicious, and they searched the moonlit night beneath, until Robbie reached the window and shoved them roughly out of the way.

'What were you doing?' he demanded furiously.

Aengus and Lizzie gaped, trying to see his face, wondering was he as angry as he sounded, and why.

'Well? Were you making wishes? You were, weren't you? And Lizzie, too, as if one wasn't enough for trouble.'

'What's wrong with you?' Aengus said. 'Lizzie pretended she was you, when Daddy came in. You haven't got anything to worry about. Daddy doesn't know you were out.'

Robbie made an impatient noise and turned to haul up the line. He threw it on the floor and closed the window.

'So what did Daddy say?' he asked shortly.

'He told me to dream up a good excuse to tell him in the morning. Why are you so mad?'

'If you'd told a good excuse tonight, you wouldn't

have to worry about the morning. You didn't tell me, either, what you were wishing.'

Difficult to exchange a glance in the dark, but Lizzie and Aengus tried. How did Robbie know they had wished?

'So what was I supposed to do,' said Aengus, 'seeing your guilty pyjamas, staring me in the face? A nice escape artist you are, flinging evidence all around. I did the only thing I could do.'

'What? Ate them?'

'I wished they'd disappear. And they did.' Aengus couldn't trust himself to say any more, he was getting vexed enough to shout. He didn't mind taking the blame for the fire escape—that was a noble thing to do—but to be blamed for keeping the blame was a bit much.

Lizzie coughed nervously, recalling all Robbie had said about wishing that morning on the bridge. She would have liked to explain how necessary were the wishes they had made, and how harmless, but that would sound too much like excuses and begging for forgiveness. Which Lizzie would scorn to do, of a brother.

'So then you wished for this, I suppose?' Robbie kicked the clothes lines.

'Being silly enough,' said Aengus, 'to think you'd want to get back in. Daddy took the fire escape with him. But I guess you're so brainy and super, you didn't need our help. And so we won't bother next time, or tomorrow, either, when the police come looking for the robber of those clothes under your bed, and the chocolate. We won't pretend we've ever heard of chocolate. You can have it all.'

'There was another wish, though,' said Robbie. 'The one that made all the noise. What was that?'

Aengus's anger was deflated by this question.

Lizzie said, 'That was me. I wished for a message from our secret guest. And you can turn up your nose, if you like,' she went on defiantly, 'and go around knowing everything, and not telling anyone, big show-off, but it's our adventure, too, we searched as hard as you did, selfish pig, and so don't try and keep it all to yourself, savage!'

There was a moment's silence. Then Robbie said, more kindly, 'You don't know what I went through, down there. You got off easy, Aengus, with just Daddy.'

He sat on the chair, knocking to the floor a stray button. Dragging something from his pocket, he silently examined it with his hands.

Aengus said. 'That's the Historic Doorknob, isn't it?'

'Tell us what happened,' Lizzie demanded.

'Give me a minute. I'm only after escaping it.'

They gave him an impatient minute, and then he told them: he had just found the doorknob, over near the stump of one of the sycamores. And then, he had heard a voice. It came out of the hawthorn hedge. He wasn't sure what it had said, or whether he had really heard it at all. When the noise of the button box had followed, he decided he had imagined it. He had hidden behind the stone seat, when the light went on in the room, and had waited to see what was happening.

Here, Robbie paused, fiddling with the doorknob. He kept his back to the eerie moonlight, the strange shadows in the familiar garden below.

He went on, then, 'While Daddy was in the room, I

34

was only thinking about how I'd get in again, and
would he know I was out. The garden's awful still and
creepy, not like our garden at all. The more I looked at
the hawthorn, the more I thought I could see something
there, something that didn't belong. And then I did
hear voices, creeping sneaking voices, like slugs if they
could talk. One said, 'Now see,' and another one said
something about open wishes, and the moon being so
bright, but not full yet. I never heard anything so
horrible.' He shuddered. 'In our garden, too, and me
without the least weapon. It wouldn't have been so bad,
if I'd been properly armed.

'Anyhow, the light went out in the room, and I really
did feel sick, stuck out in the night and the voices
sneaking along our hedge, and not knowing what they
were. I waited and waited and I thought I'd be there
forever. And then, just a little while before you threw
the line out, the voices talked again. There weren't only
two, like I'd thought, but dozens and dozens of them,
all arguing and some saying that wishes were being
made, and some agreeing and some not. And they
sneaked and creeped and made me sick, and there
wasn't a thing I could do about them.'

Lizzie and Aengus were horrified. They looked out
on the moonlit garden and could too easily imagine the
dreadful voices oozing like slugs from the shadow.

'I couldn't make out much of it,' Robbie said. 'I was
too scared, and they were all hissing at once. But I'm
sure they mentioned a "white song without words" and
"she is there and humming" and some others said she
wasn't. Some said they hadn't seen anything. When the
line came down, they shut up.'

'So she is a fugitive,' Lizzie said, 'as well as secret and lost. We've got to find and help her.'

'Sure,' Robbie said. 'But no more wishes. Those sluggy voices can see them. If they make up their minds about it, they might attack the house.'

'What about Paddy-last?' Aengus asked. 'Are we going to tell him? You know what he's like.'

'In the morning,' said Robbie. 'He's as brave as any of us, when it's bright.'

*   *   *

When Paddy-last awoke, it was to the shushing of rain and contented gabbling of Peter. Such a peaceful change, thought Paddy-last, smiling, from those bullying wake-up-and-get-up birds. Paddy-last relaxed and, unable to think of chocolate, he thought of jam.

He dreamt of shining full pots of jam, of jam easing itself onto a slice of bread, of jam quivering on a spoon. He thought of blackcurrant jam, as deeply blue as a night sky; of raspberry jam, sparkling with pips; of strawberry jam, luscious as sunset. Gooseberry jam, apricot jam, rhubarb and ginger, they paraded a glowing rainbow before his closed eyes. He went over every jam that ever was, until he was so starved, he simply had to get out of bed.

The house was sleeping quiet, not a hint of anyone else wakening. Even Lizzie, when Paddy-last climbed over her, only murmured 'geroff,' without batting an eye. This suited Paddy-last, since it meant no explanations, nor any having to share. He was forced to bring Peter, however. Peter was so thrilled to find a listener, and so heartbroken to see that listener sneaking away, that Paddy at once realized he would have to buy his silence with jam.

In the kitchen, Paddy-last began with a packet of biscuits. He gave one to Peter and ate the rest, concealing the empty wrapper behind the sink. This wasn't greed, but common sense: a half-empty packet would make his mother suspect the worst. And he would have given Peter more, if Peter had shown greater respect for the biscuit he did get. Peter was simply a waste of biscuits.

Continuing his quest, Paddy-last discovered an unopened pot of blackcurrant jam. He climbed carefully down (the jam was kept in the highest press) and tried to open it with a knife, a bottle opener, a screwdriver, and his teeth. Finally, he climbed up and climbed down again with the half pot of buttery strawberry.

'Wammer!' Peter yelled, ungratefully flinging his gnawed biscuit under the table.

'Shut up,' Paddy-last advised. 'We don't want Mammy to catch us on the brink of success.'

He cut two ragged wedges of bread and shook a portion of jam onto each. He squashed the jam about with a spoon, to spread it evenly, and handed Peter his ration. Then he simply stared to see Peter lick the jam off, and hand up the bread for more.

'Wammer,' said Peter.

'That's a good idea,' Paddy-last said. 'How did you think of it?'

He gave the baby more jam, and added another glop

to his own, to be fair. They went on until the jam was finished, and there was still plenty of bread left for breakfast. Paddy-last felt quite virtuous as he considered the nearly entire loaf.

The house remained silent except for Peter's remarks, as he squashed and rolled the ragged bread about the floor. Paddy-last was lulled by the drizzling rain, into a dream of orchestras.

The beautiful xylophone made Paddy a little scornful of his lately lamented boxes, bottlecaps, tyre tubes, and lentils. Still, one xylophone doesn't make a symphony, and it really was too bad about the wishes. He could have wished for all sorts of proper instruments, worthy to accompany the xylophone—a gleaming tin whistle, a twangy banjo, a soothing guitar, or even a grand piano. He could have assembled such an array of music, his parents would be forced to give him a room of his own, which he would call the Music Room, and keep everyone out of who didn't knock. Such a life, thought Paddy, would be one long, sweet song.

Thoughts of chocolate arose and Paddy-last sighed. 'I suppose I'll just have to make do with my xylophone, and the junk I can collect. It's awfully hard, getting enough bottle caps, when the others keep borrowing them for silly things like ships and radios and mouse dishes. If ever I got enough, I could nail them to a stick, like Aunt Ina told me. That makes a drum and tambourine all together.' He brooded on bottle caps and the difficulties of hiding them from Robbie, Aengus, and Lizzie. 'I wish,' he said thoughtlessly, 'we'd got bottle caps, a beautiful bag of bottle caps, a babble of bottle caps, a bracing—' he hushed.

From the press under the sink, came a soft chinking sound. The noise was exactly what a bagful of bottle caps would make. So much so, that Paddy-last couldn't imagine anything else. He stared at the press, his heart pounding.

When Peter heard the chinking, he had greater visions than of mere bags of bottle caps. He imagined large shining saucepans, with rolling round lids, promising lots of loud fun. Stowing his lump of bread on a chair, Peter made for the cupboard.

'Hey!' Paddy-last started out of his daze. 'They're mine!'

They raced for the press, and naturally Paddy won. He sat with his back against the door, daring Peter to howl.

'Spams,' Peter beamed winningly.

'They're mine,' said Paddy-last, immune to Peter's charms. 'Go muck about with your old bread.'

'Spams,' Peter tried again, pathetic this time.

'Go on,' Paddy-last glared heartlessly.

Peter crumpled up his face and heaved an experimental sob. He was wasting his time, for Paddy-last knew all those tricks, and despised them.

'You're not getting any,' he told the infant sternly. 'You'd only eat them. I already gave you a biscuit and jam. You can't have everything, just 'cause you're a baby.'

'Spams,' Peter mourned. He curled up to hide his face on the floor, crushed in defeat.

The cousin dealt with, Paddy now had to deal with the cupboard. He didn't like opening the door too suddenly: who knew what might jump out at him?

Would the night-noise appear in the morning? What could it do to a wish for bottle caps? Cautiously, he edged the door open a crack, and peeked in. All he could see were tea towels. He creaked it open another bit, and then swung the door wide. Nestling among the dusters was a glossy velvet bag that twinkled with gold embroidery.

Paddy-last took up the bag with trembling hands, heart thumping. Opening the drawstring of gold cord, he saw within hundreds of bottle caps, tighly packed and gleaming. Paddy-last hardly knew what to do. He simply sat, gaping at the collection, not even noticing Peter's carouse among the tea towels.

A noise of someone awake in the house finally brought Paddy to his senses. No one was going to accuse him of stealing bottle caps, but the velvet bag wasn't the sort of thing to go unremarked. And it would be a pity to go to gaol for the bag, when it was the bottle caps he had wanted.

Feverishly, he rooted through a drawerful of bills, recipes, and letters, until he found a paper bag. He poured the loot into this, and, after a panicky moment, threw the velvet bag out of the window. It fell under the holly by the door and was at once a sodden mess. Then he hid the bottle caps back in the cupboard, to avoid any questions he wasn't ready to answer.

Someone was definitely coming downstairs. Paddy-last couldn't tell who, and began snatching up the litter of towels, much to Peter's amusement. The young cousin thought this was a new game. For as many tea towels as Paddy-last managed to get back into the cupboard, the infant took out six more again.

It was a great relief, therefore, when no one worse than Uncle Conor walked in. He said, 'You should have tied the kid down, Paddy.'

*   *   *

Uncle Conor and Aunt Ina left to catch their plane after breakfast. Peter ignored their fond farewells until they had vanished into the miserable rain. Then he screamed.

Now, the children thought, at last, at last they would be free to hunt out that weird creature and get rid of her. But their mother ordered them into the dining-room.

'Stay there and do puzzles,' she said.

'And try to keep quiet,' said their father, bearing away the roaring Peter. 'We deserve some peace.'

'Keep quiet,' Paddy-last muttered. 'Why don't they tell Peter that?' He followed the others into the dining-room. 'Oh, I wanted to do the zoo,' he said, seeing Robbie spill 'Trafalgar' on to the table.

Robbie said, 'I hope we don't have to do any puzzle to the bitter end. Starting right now, we're going to get after that wish-granter, and have an adventure. I can't stand any more of this.

'And I hope you haven't been making any wishes, Paddy-last, because you'll be sorry, when you hear about last night.'

He told the story of the night's terrors in great detail, beginning with his doubts about the Historic Door-knob, going after it by fire escape, and all that followed. He described the sluggy voices as gruesomely as

41

possible, to warn Paddy off wishing forever. Paddy's face glowed with guilt and then paled with fear. When, at the finish, the phone suddenly rang in the hall, he scrambled to hide under the table.

The others listened unabashedly as their father answered the call. They heard him say: 'Hello, Jack . . . you're joking . . . oh, no . . . everything? . . . What have you done? . . . I see . . . all right, thanks.' All that the children learned from this was that the caller had been Mr Thompson, whose name was Jack.

'I was afraid it would be the police,' Lizzie said.

'How would the police suspect us?' Aengus asked. 'Magic finger prints? They'd have to find the loot first.'

'Anyhow,' Robbie said, 'even if it was them, it would only be Sergeant Quilty from the village. You don't have to say "police" like there were dozens of them on our trail.'

'They won't arrest me, anyhow,' Paddy said from under the table. 'I haven't touched anything.'

'Come out,' he was ordered and kicked.

Paddy-last took care to creep out at the far end of the table.

'You have to take up arms now, as well as us,' Robbie lectured, 'and stick by us through handcuffs and squad cars. You're the one that wanted silly wishes, when we were searching all the countryside for plain adventure. So you're in, whether you want it or not.'

'I didn't say, I didn't want, I said I didn't like,' Paddy said sulkily, 'and all I wished for was bottle caps. A xylophone's not enough for an orchestra. You always take my bottle caps, I never have enough. I want jingle sticks. I don't want illegal clothes or chocolate. I wish—'

'Don't' they all cried.

'Fish brain,' said Aengus, 'don't you see, those sneaking voices can see the wishes happening? They're watching for it. I only hope that your bottle caps haven't signalled them to attack the house.'

'They're looking for our secret magic person,' Lizzie explained further. 'Your night-noise that was in the spare room.'

'Let them have her,' Paddy-last said. 'You don't like wishes, and I don't like adventures or night-noises.'

Robbie banged the table for patience. 'We can't surrender a distressed damsel to her enemies. We have to find and rescue her.'

'So let's get down to it,' Aengus said. 'You'll be explaining to Paddy-last forever, if you want him to understand. Where do we begin?'

'First,' Robbie said, 'we have to get Mammy and Daddy to let us out of here. And then, well, I was thinking about where this thing might hide. I got a look in the spare room after Uncle Conor and Aunt Ina left, but of course it wasn't there. And then I thought about Mrs White. Were any of you ever in her house?'

They shook their heads.

'What's Mrs White got to do with it?' Aengus asked.

'Badger says she was the last of the Maddens,' Robbie said, 'and could make magic fetch and carry. Mrs White's gone now, so her magic slave must have moved somewhere. I was wondering where she hid it, in her house, because it would probably hide in the same sort of place here. See, if we knew exactly where it was, we could just tell Mammy we were going to do our puzzles there, and get right to the point.'

43

'There wasn't much to Mrs White's house,' Lizzie said. 'We'd better search everywhere.'

'I don't want to,' Paddy moaned.

'If you weren't such a coward,' Robbie told him, 'you wouldn't have to worry about getting hurt. Heroes never do. Their friends and relations do, but heroes always survive to wreak vengeance and save the day.'

'Okay,' Paddy-last said, after a moment's thought. 'I'll be a hero. Just tell me when to begin, so the adventure will recognize me and I don't get hurt by mistake.'

'So, can we start?' Aengus said.

Lizzie said, 'We'd better get rid of the clothes first. We don't want to get arrested in the middle of a dangerous assignment. They're all plain and ordinary clothes, so whoever they belong to will call the police.'

'You can't be a hero if the police arrest you,' Paddy-last said with dismay. 'And we never had to brave the police before, so how can we know what to do? I wish the clothes would go back where they came from, so we could just be heroes, and not robbers. Uncle Fergus says,' he quoted to prove all he said, 'it's better to face the music you know, so you can sing along, and Daddy says he'd know, so you can't tell me he was only teasing me and telling lies, if Daddy says he was right.' He looked around the table and, seeing accusing stares, added defiantly, 'Well, I'm not going to be a robber, anyhow. Go be one yourselves.'

After a pained silence, Robbie said, 'It's a waste of time talking to you.'

Lizzie said, 'Fat mouth.'

Aengus said, 'I'll go check.'

He ran upstairs and looked under the beds. No bundled clothes were present, though the line and pegs remained. Poking around to make quite sure, Aengus noticed that the bags they had filled with chocolate gave an un-chocolate, metallic sound. He dragged one out, with a lot of pulling, for it had grown strangely heavy. Looking in, he found bottle caps. A quick feel proved that all the chocolate had been traded in.

'This is great,' Aengus said to himself. 'We're turning into a robber's warehouse. Quick delivery a speciality.'

There was a noise from the stairs. Aengus pushed the heavy bags out of sight and ran out onto the landing. As he went, his mind raced with excuses for being outside the dining-room bounds. He didn't come up with a decent one, nor need one: Peter was the noise, creeping up one step at a time. His hands were jammed with bread, and behind him trailed a line of sticky crumbs.

'Where are you going?' Aengus asked, as though the baby were able to answer.

Peter ignored him. He was tackling the steps in a business-like way, muttering reassurances to the wads of bread. The Great Explorer in Aengus was roused. He stepped back into the doorway, to observe the phenomenon.

On the landing, Peter tottered to his feet. He stood a moment, swaying, moulding the bread and murmuring comfort to it. When his legs were steady, he staggered on, until he was directly under the attic hatch. Aengus watched Peter begin a curious performance.

'Fabbitmoon,' said the infant, looking up and waving the bread. 'Baffit mooooon!' He craned his neck until his balance was overset, causing him to sit down suddenly. Peter went on calling, however, sometimes 'fabbitmoon', and sometimes, 'baffitmoon'.

Aengus, breathless, fixed his eyes on the attic hatch, waiting for the appearance of Peter's mission. That's where our magic fugitive is, he thought. It must have asked Peter to feed it, when they met in the linen closet the day before. Wait until the others hear this! They wouldn't cast such scorn on a proven comrade in arms.

No appearance occurred, however. Peter's call was broken by the phone's ringing again. Aengus suddenly remembered he was supposed to be in the dining-room. He ran out and snatched up and gagged the infant, and listened.

'Hello,' his father was saying into the phone. 'What! Well, that's a surprise . . . I've never heard the like . . . that's true . . . okay, goodbye, Jack.' He hung up the phone, and called, 'Who's up there?'

Aengus un-gagged Peter, who came on like an alarm. He ran down and shoved the gooey infant at his father, and said, 'I heard him creeping about. He went upstairs all by himself!' and swiftly escaped into the dining-room.

Leaning against the closed door, panting dramatically, Aengus announced, 'I know where she is. She's in the attic.' He described Peter's antics, exaggerating to make sure he was believed.

The others were reluctant to give Peter any credit.

'He mightn't have meant anything by it,' Lizzie said. 'He was maybe only pretending.'

Aengus said, 'Babies don't pretend. They mean what they do.'

Paddy-last droned a new song for the occasion:

'What a baby means to do
Isn't what I'd mean, or you.
Babies have mysterious minds
That run in circles
round our lines.'

'And look', Paddy added, 'at all the trouble he got me into this morning, with his bread on the chair. Didn't mean any harm by it, or anything, but it's all the same.'

'That's right,' Robbie said. 'I'm not going to strain all my fibres getting into the forbidden attic, only to find that the infant didn't mean any harm. We've already had enough trouble this morning, explaining the fire escape and helping Paddy out of his jam. And look at our future: dragging Peter along all the highways and byways of adventure, besides taking his advice, heh, heh.'

'So you're not even going to try?' Aengus said.

'How?' Lizzie said reasonably. 'The attic's forbidden ground, ever since Paddy fell through the hatch. And we're all in such disgrace now, with fire escapes and jam, they're not likely to do us any favours.'

'You're not in disgrace,' Aengus pointed out. 'You can ask.'

'No,' Lizzie said. 'Just because I'm not in disgrace, doesn't mean I want to be.'

Paddy-last, concentrating on a misplaced piece of puzzle sky, said, 'We could have a brilliant chariot race up there. The old pushchair is there, and the plastic tractor that Robbie wouldn't share when he got too big for it, and Peter's chariot is light, we could carry it up. I wouldn't mind a chariot race.'

After a surprised silence, Aengus said, 'That's it. That's what we'll do: have a chariot race in here, and when they complain, we'll come up with the attic, casual-like.'

'And then what do you think they'll say?' Robbie asked. 'They'll say: we told you to do your stupid puzzles.'

'Let's try,' Lizzie switched sides. 'It wouldn't hurt, and it's a shame to waste a good plan like that, especially one that Paddy-last helped in. He never has good ideas.'

'All right,' Robbie agreed. 'I suppose we should encourage him. I'll fetch Peter's chariot. We'll probably break it, or break something, seeing as it's partly Paddy's idea, but what harm? At least we won't hear any more about phenomenal comrades in arms.'

The pushchair was in the hall closet. As Robbie extracted it, very carefully, he could hear his parents in the kitchen. They were discussing Thompson's clothes line. With horror, he heard his mother say, 'I wish our laundry would disappear as handy.'

'I wish it wouldn't!' Robbie wished in a hurry. 'I wish nobody would wish anything!'

At once, there was a noise, like a piano being flung down the stairs. Robbie's hand was on the pushchair and he thought, at first, he had knocked some of the precariously perched junk that lived in the closet. But nothing there had moved.

Of course, his parents appeared. They had a sudden magic of their own, when illegal noises happened.

'I was just getting the pushchair,' Robbie said, before they could accuse. 'We're going to have a chariot race.'

'Not in the dining-room,' his mother said, forgetting the piano din that had brought her out.

'How about the attic, then?' Robbie casually croaked. He cleared his throat. 'We—Paddy thought you might let us play in the attic.'

'No,' said his mother, but his father said, 'They might as well. There's no better place, for putting them out of sight and sound. But you had better leave Peter's pushchair here. You'll break it.'

'Okay,' Robbie said, hardly able to believe his luck.

While his father went upstairs to arrange the ladder to the hatch, Robbie fetched his brothers and sister. He also hopefully fetched the sword from above his bed, for if Paddy's plans could work, so might babies be meaningful.

CHAPTER 4

In the Old Pushchair

Fewer places could appear so calmly bare of adventure as did the attic. When Aengus had carefully closed the hatch as he had been instructed, he stood, with his brothers and sister, in a tight knot, staring around the blankly echoing spaces.

The attic wasn't exactly empty. At intervals across the board floor were boxes of school books, bagged clothes, heaped Christmas decorations, and a great coil of wire. A long roll of carpet lay beneath the dormer windows to the front. It was thick with dust, as were the wide sunbeams that slanted across the glowing gloom. Shoved behind one of the chimneys, which rose like pillars from floor to ceiling, were the dingy orange toy tractor, and the clumsy old pushchair.

It was on the old pushchair that the expectant gazes came to rest. This huge and awkward contraption was practically an antique, having begun its career with Robbie and worked its way down through Paddy-last. It had a heavy canopy, a folding bag at the back, and a basket slung beneath. Across the front was a string of parti-coloured elephants, which jingled when shook. The old pushchair of smothering canvas and scratched enamel seemed strangely large, compared to Peter's neat little chariot. The more the children stared, the stranger the old pushchair appeared.

Lizzie was the first to realize that there was someone sitting in the ancient heirloom. As soon as she made out the dim and dusty figure, she recognized a true outcast: rather wild, probably homeless, and certainly without friends. In other words, there sat the equal to any beleaguered badger or forlorn frog.

Paddy-last saw the shape and dared sigh with relief. It was only the wretched night-noise, after all, uglier than ever without its green glow. He didn't have to start being a hero yet.

Aengus doubted the worth of whatever civilization this castaway had wandered from, while Robbie with surprise saw distress without a proper damsel.

The distressed occupant of the old pushchair didn't see the children at once, so they took time to look over her spidery-thin arms and legs, her sharp, pasty face, her huge black eyes, and her mat of dirty yellow hair. She wore an untidy bunching of grimy silk and creased satin, all trimmed with tarnished tinsel. On her feet were a pair of high-laced boots, that were creaking new and certainly the only decent thing about her. She was absorbed in reading an old comic, one of a pile on her lap. With each page she turned, she sniffed.

Once Lizzie was satisfied she had found a wild friend, she led the way across the bare floor.

'What are you reading?' she asked sociably.

'Oh!' the distressed reader cried out, horribly startled. She flung the comic into the air, rolling her eyes until they seemed ready to pop out. The elephants jingled madly.

'Don't be scared,' Aengus soothed her. 'We've come to rescue you from a dreadful doom.'

Paddy-last picked up the comic. 'It's an old one,' he said, turning the pages. 'It's one of those Uncle Fergus gave us, when we had the mumps. He threw them through the window and broke my jar of bees.'

'Show me,' Lizzie snatched. 'There was a story about squirrels in one of these. You didn't find it, did you?'

The distressed creature gaped wordlessly, her face pale beneath the grime.

'She doesn't look a bit magic,' Paddy-last criticized. 'Was it really you that took my orchestra?'

'Don't talk rubbish,' Aengus said, shoving him. 'She's still scared. We're your rescuers,' he repeated, slowly so that the glad tidings could penetrate. 'This is Robbie the sword bearer. That's Lizzie, friend of the wild. I'm Aengus, starless navigator and map-maker. And Paddy is our brother. Who are you?'

She turned her wide gaze on Robbie, who was the only one yet to speak. She seemed especially fascinated by the sword he held. Addressing him, she said, 'By Pocket have I long been known, in pockets found a name and home. Welcome, O Heroes, with your greetings strange, your words of doom, your many names.'

Robbie had been stifling a laugh, unable to speak up to now. The dingy, feeble creature, reading old comics in an older pushchair, and then Aengus's attempts to treat her as a true adventure, were all wildly funny. She looked like a fairy left over from a school play. But she had a voice of purest music, a voice which invited the sympathy of any real hero.

'You didn't know', he said, 'that you're in danger?'

'Unwary prey!' Lizzie whispered with a thrill.

'Pocket,' Paddy said. 'She can talk after all.'

Pocket, if that was her name, and she seemed to think it was, looked all around the attic. Seeing nothing more threatening than a wasp bouncing against a window, she turned her wide eyes to Robbie, mutely questioning.

'Danger gathers,' Robbie said with relish, 'beneath the mooncast shadow of the hawthorn. Spying voices lurk therein, whispering betrayal of a wordless song!'

Paddy-last complained, 'Don't start talking like that, Robbie, or I won't know what's going on at all.'

More business-like, Aengus suggested, 'Let's all sit down, and hear her tale of woe, and we can tell her ours, and find out what's to be done.'

'Okay,' they all agreed, settling down on the hard floor around the pushchair. They looked to Pocket with eager hope.

Pocket looked back, bewildered. Then she laughed. 'Frogs,' she said. 'Frogs with brightly solemn eyes!'

'What do you mean?' Paddy-last said, outraged.

'Shh!' Lizzie elbowed him.

Pocket cringed, scared all over again. 'Your pardon, I beg, may I never offend the roof that shelters. Would that I had a tale of woe to favour you, as you have favoured me. Alas, I am but a torn page, without beginning or end, no tale have I but of pockets, and of pockets again: imprisoning pockets deeply vile. Is this a tale meet for heroes? Of pockets dark and wishes drear?'

'No,' said Lizzie. 'But you're not in a pocket now, so I guess you weren't in one to begin with.'

'Where did you come from?' asked Aengus.

'Where are you going?' asked Robbie.

Paddy-last kept his question to himself, as he wondered whether they would be done with this crazy lady in time for a chariot race. Having prepared himself to heroically survive an adventure, all there was to survive was this Pocket, who was plainly bananas. Frogs, indeed! Paddy felt cheated.

Pocket leaned back in the pushchair, rolling her gaze up to its canopy. Her mouth turned upside-down. After some thought, she said softly:

'Pockets and pockets and pockets again, deep as years of greedy gathering. And then, an awakening. A cold still room, a castle of grey ash, falling to dust. And through a window, a twinkling of stars! That is the first part,' Pocket murmured, speaking so low, the children strained to hear. 'For the second part, hard roads ground by cold metal hedgerows, held in cold abeyance; a cold, hard world, for a befuddled wanderer such as I. Terrors upon terrors, a pebble idly gathered, idly let fall, set rolling helplessly down deep gorges. And the third part, or is it the first?'

She sat up. Her black eyes were as flat and round as dishes, as she fixed them unwinking on Robbie's sword. 'I heard my name called,' she said. 'Not "Pocket", but a name I know nothing of, nor can I now recall, save that it is my own. I followed that call, and though its beckoning is now forgotten, I wait here, within its reach.'

'Here?' Robbie said. 'It brought you here?'

'There's got to be more to it than that,' said Aengus restlessly. 'Where were you, before the pockets?'

Pocket passed trembling hands over her face. 'Please,' she said. 'The dreadful flame. The terrible fire.'

'She's bananas,' Paddy-last scoffed.

'And you're nuts,' said Lizzie. 'Leave her alone.'

'I haven't touched her,' Paddy-last said indignantly.

Pocket kept murmuring, 'Please,' making quite a melody of her petition.

'Okay,' said Robbie. 'One: did you grant those wishes?'

Pocket admitted timidly, 'Rather, did this husk of grey desires do so.'

'Two, then: what was that noise, when I was getting the chariot, I mean, Peter's pushchair out of the closet? Just after I un-wished Mammy's wish about the laundry.'

'Wasn't that you?' Lizzie asked him.

Pocket spoke over Lizzie's words, saying, 'Oh, but that was you! All of you! What powers do you possess, who wield a sword of heaven's fire? For this spacious chamber filled with lights, dancing, dancing to a music I had never known lost. You restored my voice! You wished me well, you did, indeed, you did,' she said, as if they meant to deny it. 'So, did you restore my voice, but what must be wished, to restore my very self?'

She grasped the parti-coloured elephants in a white-knuckled hold, her flat eyes beseeching earnestly.

'The Historic Doorknob,' Lizzie said, nudging Robbie. 'Go get it. I have an idea.'

'So have I,' said Robbie. 'Hang on.'

He ran for the hatch, shoved it clattering aside and flew down the ladder. He ran into his room, snatched up the Historic Doorknob, and ran back to the ladder.

He fairly rocketed into the attic, quick enough to prevent Aengus and Paddy's beginning to ask, what idea?

'Try that,' Robbie said. He held out the doorknob.

Pocket snatched it eagerly. The children watched her close examination, with bated breaths. Now they were getting somewhere, they thought, as Pocket muttered and squinted unattractively over the old glass.

She was ages, however, in her investigation. If indeed they were getting anywhere, the journey there seemed to require much thought from Pocket. Paddy-last grew bored and began to long for a chariot race. Robbie fidgetted with disappointment, having expected instant and dramatic results. Only Aengus and Lizzie waited patiently, taking interest in Pocket's curious behaviour. They were the first to see the change which finally stilled Robbie, and stayed Paddy-last in his furtive edging towards the plastic tractor.

A faint whiff of magic pervaded the dustily sun-beamed attic. Some deeper power, some greater gift than the bestowal of button boxes, clothes lines, and bottle caps, hummed within the dingy Pocket. Her earlier cringing flaked like dried mud, as she began to recognize herself for what she had been long, long ago.

Speaking into the doorknob, as though reading, she said: 'A legend is this, nay, but a dream, spun as the night falls, as the hour of quiet descends to hush the winged songs of day. Yet the curlew cries out her melancholy name from the wet lands beyond the iron-bound hearths. Into this soft evening, strays the daughter of Lisgaoth.

'Fair daughter of the winds,' Pocket murmured.

'Before her gold-clad footfall starts a waft of amber wings: they seek the unrisen moon. And the silver-haired, the emerald-eyed, the ivory daughter of Lisgaoth, hastens to gather the reflections in Oranbeg, ere the moon drowns the diamond points in liquid gold.

'See Lisgaoth, fort of the winds, crown of the green hill!

'And see below, Brunabawn, palace stronghold of Eoin Whitehand, the beloved of Lisgaoth's fair daughter.

'Yet what is this, which glitters grey, pours forth from beyond the hill? A cold torrent of spears, a chilling call of battle. Greybranch leads Torkeel to war. Greybranch seeks to bind with silver chains the white singer of Lisgaoth!

'Torkeel: grey tangle of webs, shadows without pattern, silver without song. Torkeel: thriving on the witless unwanted wanderers. Torkeel: discordant throng who seek to steal concord in song, to beat into measure, phrased in chains, clad in grey undertones and uncoloured refrains!

'And Greybranch—' Pocket gulped, her face creasing with fear. 'Greybranch.' She shuddered and paused.

The children waited in suspense, while Pocket gasped and panted like a runner trying to catch her breath to impart a vital message.

'Now,' Pocket continued, still raggedly breathing, 'now, what of the daughter of Lisgaoth? Fleeing the swift river of Torkeel, dare she the iron-bound hearths, the bitter roads of mankind? Oh, foolish daughter though fair, she strays too early among the grasping hands. See: one reaches out and captures the darting beam of song. Ah, to trespass before nightfall, the cold-furrowed fields, is folly deserving the coldest fate!'

The silence which followed was complete. Pocket sat rigid—in terror—and the children held their breaths, waiting to hear the end of the tale. But there was no end to it. A tractor roaring past in the road below, started Pocket upright. The elephants jangled and she laughed.

'You restored my voice, and now, you open my eyes! Daughter of Lisgaoth indeed I was, and am. Of silver hair, of emerald eyes, the ivory daughter of Lisgaoth. But what becomes of an harp neglected? Or of a precious vessel employed in feeding swine? Broken and defiled, heavy with filth. Ah, a granter of wishes, now, yes, you behold the result. What you see here sends forth the stench of greed, not I, not the buried daughter of Lisgaoth!'

She spoke passionately, squeezing the doorknob between her bony hands. The children didn't know how to respond. Somehow, without changing her appearance, Pocket was no longer the meekly distressed damsel, but an imperious though fugitive queen. Without laying down any plans of action she had taken command.

She said now, 'Within this opening star, smeared by some mortal magic, much is dimly writ. I see myself, I see the door of Brunabawn, I see the door regathered and opened to avenge the hills. Tell me all,' she demanded of the children. 'Reveal to me the meaning of the scattered door, of Lisgaoth so strangely silent, of this muddled spell that dims the light of purer magic.'

They all stared at her blankly.

'What do you mean?' Robbie asked crossly. 'You're

the one who's supposed to know everything. All we know is, well . . .' His voice trickled away in embarrassment. He was annoyed with himself, and with Pocket for overstepping the part of distressed damsel.

Aengus cleared his throat. 'About Brunabawn,' he said.

'What about it?' Robbie asked shortly.

'It's that mound, beyond the ruined cottages,' Aengus said. 'The one young Mr MacAdam told me is really a glacial deposit. And Torkeel, that's an old wood, about a mile beyond the hill. I'm not putting it on the map of local lost civilizations, because it's not really local to us, you know, but I am putting an arrow pointing to it.'

'Brilliant,' Robbie said. 'So what? We were all over Brunabawn, when we were looking for adventure. And what did we get? Nettle stings, and Paddy-last ran from a cow. A cow!' He glared rudely at Pocket, blaming her for being a riddle, and not an answer.

'Don't you start calling names,' Lizzie fired up. 'I don't care, she's my wild friend, now, so you just watch what you say. You leave my wild friends alone.'

'With pleasure,' Robbie said.

Aengus turned to Pocket. 'You mentioned a door to Brunabawn.'

Pocket said, 'A door of gold, fixed by a single star, swung on a song of silver, ringing with joy.'

'Sit still, a minute, Robbie, will you?' Aengus said. 'Paddy-last!'

'I'm not doing nothing,' Paddy-last said, jumping.

'How do you get wishes from a fairy?'

'No such thing,' Paddy said warily.

59

'Yes, but what did the egg woman tell you? You know, when she told you about cold iron being deadly.'

'Oh, her,' said Paddy-last. 'She told me, if you catch a fairy and keep it in your pocket, and don't tell anyone, then it has to grant your wishes. I don't believe it, I didn't ask her, she just told me freely of her own will, and gave me a small brown egg for myself.'

'Listen, Robbie,' said Aengus, 'young Mr MacAdam told me this story about local lost civilizations: see, there used always be raids between different tribes, and one day Torkeel raided Drumanaar, that old fort at the top of the hill. And the crowd from Brunabawn would have helped the gang in Drumanaar, only Torkeel went and stole their door, so they couldn't get out. I've never heard of any Lisgaoth, but Drumanaar means something like "the fort of weeping, or mourning", or something sad like that. And no wonder. It's smashed flat.'

Robbie whistled slowly.

Lizzie gulped a couple of times and asked, 'Was Pocket kidnapped, then? And kept in pockets to grant wishes for, why, the Maddens! The Maddens that Mrs White was the last of. And now Pocket is so mixed up,' she concluded tenderly, 'from granting dull wishes about cows and things, that she can't remember her own name.'

'And the night she was kidnapped,' said Robbie, 'must be the night when the door was swiped, too. And our Historic Doorknob belonged to it! Imagine!'

The children stared hungrily at Pocket. Only Paddy-last said, 'That's silly. People don't kidnap fairies, fairies kidnap people, or they would if I believed in them. And anyhow, she wasn't in our pockets when she granted all those wishes, and that doorknob is our heirloom. Let's have a chariot race,' he whined. 'That's why I wanted to come up here, only you made a plan out of my own idea. I want a race.'

He was ignored, of course.

'So, where's the rest of the door?' Robbie asked Aengus. 'Are all the good guys trapped in Brunabawn, or did someone let them out?'

Aengus shrugged. 'I forget. It was on my map, the one the magic tidied away. But we can ask young Mr MacAdam.'

'Would you like that?' Lizzie asked Pocket. 'Would you like us to get the door and let you into Brunabawn? Or would you rather go some place else? Or stay here? You could stay here and be my resident friend.'

'She can't stay here,' Robbie said shortly. 'Isn't that why we came looking for her, to get rid of her?'

Lizzie said, 'I thought we came to rescue her.'

'Same thing.'

'It isn't.'

'Of course it is. Distressed damsels are always got rid of, once they're rescued.'

Aengus said, 'You're not giving Pocket much of a chance to talk. But can't you stop the wishes?' he asked Pocket. 'Is it a habit, or what? Because we'd rather you didn't.'

'You fret over wishes,' Pocket said, 'and you squabble and you whine. So much for mortal magic,' said she, vigorously rubbing the doorknob with the tattered silk, 'mortal magic, that casts nets to snare small fry,' she sneered.

'The door is mine to command,' she told them, 'and therefore you, the doorkeepers, are under my orders. By all means visit this learned friend, and discover whatever may be of use to my quest. For plainly we must recover the door, and release vengeance upon Greybranch and all Torkeel, if they do not bring us to battle before. And do you mislike wishes, make none.'

'You're so smart,' Paddy-last said resentfully. 'If you knew as much as you think you do, you wouldn't be so smart! Huh, us recover a door and fight Greybranch. Is that all? Can't think of anything else?'

'Like what?' Robbie, Aengus, and Lizzie wondered. And secretly they hoped that Paddy had a good answer, for not even the friend of wild things likes to be told she squabbles and whines and is under orders.

'Like sneaky voices,' Paddy-last reminded them. 'Creeping about our garden, looking for her. Is she going to fix them, or isn't she, or can she at all?'

'Voices!' Pocket leaned forward, her round eyes making Paddy-last regret he'd spoken.

Robbie took command, most grateful for the chance to do so. He told Pocket, 'It's how we figured out you were needing our help. I went out into the garden to fetch the Historic Doorknob, and while I was out, the others had to make wishes. And every time they did, I heard voices, hiding in the hawthorn.' Robbie went on, into greater detail, when he saw the horror which froze Pocket's arrogance into a grimace of fear. He couldn't help it: she had taken over their adventure, and had reduced four heroes to the role of mere servants, paltry doorkeepers. Her cool assumption of authority couldn't be fairly argued with, so Robbie argued unfairly. He even took advantage of Pocket's evident fear of his sword, by waving it in her face as he spoke.

When the tale was ended, Lizzie said, 'You didn't have to make it so creepy. I guess she knows herself how scarey it is. Didn't she have all Torkeel chase her?'

'That's nothing,' said Paddy-last. 'She couldn't be as scared of them as we are. She knows what they are, doesn't she?'

'The p'tain,' Pocket hissed, 'the p'tain of Torkeel. The battle begins so soon!'

She climbed awkwardly out of the pushchair, making the elephants jangle. Comics littered the floor about her ungainly booted feet. She stood as tall as she could, which wasn't much taller than Paddy. Skinny and dingy, she clutched the Historic Doorknob to her chest.

'Harken to my counsel,' she demanded in her beautiful voice. 'This night let you abandon speech, to embrace deeds. These secret voices must be silenced forever. You shall do this when the waxing moon rises: driving them forth from their shadows, you shall smite them with brilliance.'

The children considered the command in their various ways, none of them daring to refuse the urgency and the authority of the determined Pocket. She was irresistible.

Lizzie asked, 'Will they still be spying, if we go after them? Maybe they've gone back to report.'

'That's not how stories go,' Robbie said. 'They'll be there.'

'This isn't a story, really,' quavered Paddy.

'But adventures always are like stories,' Aengus said.

'Look at the Great Explorers' stories that really happened.'

'Oh, yeah?' said Paddy-last. 'What about the Great Explorers that never come back?'

'We'll draw straws,' Robbie broke in, 'bits of paper, because we can't all go. I mean, we're going to have to wait until after Mammy and Daddy are gone to bed. I'm not keen on fire escapes. I'd rather chance sneaking out the kitchen door, and you know that four of us can't sneak.'

'How many, then,' Aengus said.

'Two. The two shortest straws will go. I'll hold them and take whatever is left.'

The first draw was Paddy-last's, who wanted to choose while he could be sure there were at least two long ones in the fold. His choice was a short straw.

Aengus and Lizzie pulled together, a long straw each. They were dreadfully disappointed.

So was Paddy-last. Robbie didn't know how he felt.

Robbie asked, 'What's the best thing to fight these p'tain with?'

'You are already armed,' Pocket said. 'You brandish a sword tempered with fire from stormy skies. What greater protection do you desire, against the hidden people and their minions?'

Robbie gazed along the length of his sword. It was merest wood, painted silver, made from a blasted branch from a lightning-struck tree. He had made it out of the handiest materials he could get, and was pleased, now, to learn that he couldn't have chosen better.

'Sword Lightstriker,' he said. 'That's what I'll call it from now on.'

'What about me?' said Paddy-last, mouth wobbling. 'I don't got nothing.'

'Be of good heart, you shall triumph, I swear,' said Pocket. 'One of four stalwart heroes, you can do no less.'

'Can't I?'

Lizzie kindly offered, 'If you don't want to, Padders, I'll go.'

'That's not fair,' Aengus protested. 'I want to go, too.'

'Paddy-last is going,' said Robbie. 'He'll be okay,' he added doubtfully. 'After all, he met Pocket first.'

Pocket counselled, 'Keep your fury for the foe, and in peace prepare. Heroes never wrangle thusly for honour.'

'Don't they?' Lizzie said. 'We always do.'

Their mother's voice, calling, broke in on the council, to let them know that it was a quarter to one, did they want their lunch or not?

'We're coming,' Aengus called back.

'Don't disappear,' Lizzie told Pocket. 'You have to be in the vanguard with me and Aengus.'

'With the left-over heroes,' said Aengus.

*　　*　　*

Robbie would have liked to spend the afternoon preparing Paddy-last to meet the foe. However, the children's parents had the bright idea of going for a drive, which not only prevented preparation, but quite ruined all attempts at peace. There was something about the back of a car, which inclined the four heroes to quarrelling. With Peter added, so was the noise and the reasons for rowing.

Because of the rows, and because of all the minor crimes of the night and morning, the children were sent early to bed. The older ones thought this was a good idea, as they hadn't had much sleep the night before, and weren't likely to get any tonight, once the moon rose. But they found there was no hope of sleeping. From seven o'clock until near midnight, when Pocket came to warn them of the moonrise, the children all lay drowsily awake.

Aengus and Lizzie were kept awake by plain envy. Neither of them begrudged Robbie his share of the glory. After all, the voices were his discovery. But they did resent being done out of adventure by Paddy. He might have met Pocket first, but he hadn't known what she was, nor wanted to know.

Paddy himself was kept awake in a rather doubtful state; torn between joy and fear. He was going to be a hero, and he was scared to death. How could he combat those voices? Should he ask Aengus for the rubber knife? Or borrow a real one from the kitchen? Ought he to make a last-minute search for an iron talisman? But everything likely had been tidied away, by Pocket herself.

All Robbie worried about was Paddy-last.

Pocket went to Aengus first, surprising him out of a doze of maps. The sight of Pocket, glowing pale in the darkness, exactly fitted in with the doze. Her glow was quite horrible. She reminded him of the luminous skeleton Uncle Fergus had given them last Hallowe'en. He wondered if, after all, he had fallen asleep.

'They are without,' she announced, 'skulking beneath the walls of thorn. Rouse the valorous, oh starless
one.'

'Don't talk so loud,' Aengus cautioned. 'Daddy will
hear.'

With amusement, Pocket said, 'Who can hear, but he
who listens? Arise, make haste, the moon flies to her
zenith.'

Aengus got out of bed, stifling a yell as he trod on a
forgotten button. He could hear Robbie getting up, and
went to fetch Lizzie and Paddy-last. Robbie followed
with the glowing Pocket. She gave Paddy-last an awful
start.

No one said anything. The house was darkly quiet,
untouched by any noise from outside, for all the world
was silent. That was the worst of the country, thought
Paddy: in the city, there was always traffic to keep you
company.

He and Robbie crept away down the stairs. Aengus
and Lizzie moved back to the boys' room, which was
farther from their parents', and therefore safer.

'Why do you glow like that?' Lizzie asked with
distaste of Pocket.

'And why do you not?' Pocket asked in return, her
smile most hideous for her ghostly light.

'Where did you put the doorknob?' Aengus wanted
to know. 'I hope you're minding it.'

Pocket didn't reply, but floated to one of the windows. She didn't exactly fly, yet she didn't walk, and
had she been as beautiful as every damsel has a right to
be, the graceful skimming would have thrilled. As she
was, glowing greenly beneath the grime, the gentle

drifting motion only showed her worse than she was.

Aengus and Lizzie looked at her for a moment, before going to watch from a different window. They were uneasy with her, confused about her place in the adventure, and about their own places besides. Her authority put them out, as did her making them into doorkeepers. Doorkeepers! Aengus the pathfinder, and Lizzie, the friend of all wild things!

'I suppose it will work out,' Aengus murmured.

Meanwhile, below in the kitchen, Robbie paused by the back door to ask Paddy whether he was ready.

'Yes,' said Paddy-last, 'only I haven't got a weapon.'

'Then get one, quietly.'

Paddy-last tip-toed blindly across the dark room. He collided with a chair, with the table, and finally cannoned into the sink. He felt about for the cutlery drawer, searching high and low, being too wrought to search in between.

'Can't find it,' he whispered, anguish giving his voice a squeak. 'Can't you turn on the light?'

'No. Hurry. Anything will do.'

Paddy-last blundered on. His hands found many things, none of which he could identify except the kettle, for it was still warm. Then he came across a tall plastic thing, and he remembered: Robbie had described the voices as slug-like. Paddy-last filled his pockets with salt.

'Right,' he breathed, fumbling his way back to Robbie. 'I'm ready for anything now.'

Robbie eased back the bolt, turned the key, and edged the door open. They slipped out, leaving the door ajar, and they huddled together shivering on the step outside. They hadn't dressed for adventure, to avoid delay, and to be entirely innocent, if a parent did happen to catch them out. Their mother would believe a tale of hunger, and might even excuse it, so long as they weren't dressed to go out. That would look too suspicious. But the summer night was chilly, and they were soon clenching their teeth against it.

After their hands and feet were grown numb with cold, Robbie began wondering how they were supposed to find the lurking spies? How drive them out of the shadows? When Pocket declared, 'They are without,' Robbie had assumed he would at least hear them. But the garden was as black and as still as an ancient mossbound rock. There wasn't even a breeze to stir the shadows to life. The moonlight, casting a cold white swathe of gauze across the lawn, revealed nothing but the glistening dew.

So they waited, shivering more violently with every minute that passed. Robbie kept a frozen hand on the hilt of Sword Lightstriker. Paddy-last's two fists were in his dressing gown pockets, and crammed with salt.

Above, Aengus and Lizzie waited too, and wondered what was, or wasn't happening. They got pains in their necks, their hands fell asleep, and their legs tingled with the strain of not running down to help their brothers.

At the next window waited Pocket, humming softly. She didn't seem worried, but pleased with herself. As well she might, having been a slave to wishes for so long.

The hush, deeper than the usual night quiet,

stretched on and on, like a super elastic band. And at last, it snapped with a prolonged hissing.

Paddy-last let go of one fistful of salt, to grab Robbie's arm. The hissing hadn't been needed to alert them to what they saw: something vague and stickily glistening oozed from the shadow of the hawthorn. Slimily rippling across the wet grass, the p'tain raised round pale eyes to the house, as they moved slowly, but without hesitation, towards it.

Two led the uneasily creeping company, followed by four, six, eight, ten more. The watching children experienced an awfully unheroic feeling at the sight. They felt sick, frightened, and angry all at once, as they watched the sluggish band of unblinking pale eyes creep across *their* back garden, seeking out, of all, *their* house.

Spurred on by the anger, which overcame his sickness and fear, Robbie moved at last. Bounding forth into the moonlight, he dragged Paddy along with him. And as he raised Sword Lightstriker, Paddy-last lost hold of his arm and was flung, staggering, right to the edge of shadow.

Sweeping his blade down in a chopping motion, Robbie thudded among the pale eyes, putting them out as he went. The bodies thrashed convulsively, as the round glares faded. Some touched Robbie's bare feet, leaving a cold slime.

By the hawthorn, Paddy set about in panic. Desperate with fright, and without the least notion of daring deeds, he plunged his hands into his pockets, and scattered salt. He didn't even aim, and with the p'tain thick underfoot, he didn't have to.

The effect of the salt simply terrified Paddy the more. The p'tain wriggled smoking beneath the shower, crying out horribly, like lamenting seagulls, like creaking doors, like wind trapped in a chimney. Scared as he was, Paddy-last turned in meaningless circles, flinging the salt as he gibbered with fear.

Aengus and Lizzie squeezed each other, as horrified and as helpless as Paddy. The waxing moonlight was filling with a grey fog, and the terrible noises that came from the sluggish mist told them nothing. Soon, neither Robbie nor Paddy-last nor the ambushed spies were visible from the window. If terror hadn't rooted them to the spot, the two onlookers would have thundered down the stairs and into the fog of battle below.

Eventually, the cries died away, after a long moment of frozen time, leaving a dead body of silence. The fog swirled greasily, shuddering, and then suddenly vanishing. Aengus and Lizzie almost wept with relief to see Robbie and Paddy-last still standing. Well, not exactly standing, either: Robbie was stumbling about, using his sword as a crutch, and Paddy was still jerking out handfuls of salt that fell with a sandy swish on the leaves of the hawthorn.

'Will we fetch them in?' Lizzie whispered.

'Let's,' Aengus agreed.

They ignored Pocket, or forgot about her, or didn't see her still glowing by her window. Sneaking down the stairs on trembling legs, they made their way to the kitchen. Lizzie switched on the light there, and Aengus didn't object. The homely scene was exactly what was needed. Just a glance at the familiar room gave them the strength to go through to the garden.

Outside, Aengus caught Paddy-last's arms and propelled him indoors. Lizzie led Robbie away by the
hand. The ground under their bare feet was thickly
sticky, but that was all the evidence of the late battle, or
of the vanquished p'tain.

In the kitchen, Robbie and Paddy-last came out of
their daze with the suddenness of an awakening. From
the chill moonlit garden, to the brilliantly plain kitchen
was an abrupt, complete, and welcome change.

Robbie slumped onto a chair, but Paddy-last, after
blinking once or twice, grinned at the refrigerator, so
neat and modern and unadventurous. 'Amn't I a hero,
now,' he asked it. 'Heroes always get feasted after their
victories.'

'All right,' said Aengus. 'Mammy won't mind, if we
eat real food, and not just jam.'

'It's three o'clock,' Robbie noted. 'I wonder what time
it all began? Seems ages but only a small while ago, if
you know what I mean.'

'I do,' Lizzie said. 'We thought you'd never start the
battle, but once it began, it all seemed too sudden. I'll
make toast.'

'I'll make cocoa,' said Aengus, 'and there's cream,
too, if Daddy didn't use it all in his coffee.'

'I'll see,' volunteered Paddy-last, running to embrace
the refrigerator.

Robbie scraped the black parts of the toast and
buttered what was left. He sprinkled on sugar and
cinnamon, so as to not be too sensible. After all, they
were celebrating a victory, and that can't be done
without something extravagant.

Gathered about the table to dig in, they forgot the

hour and chatted with lively interruptions, crossing each other to describe each their own reactions to the battle. Paddy-last wavered between the glory of heroism, and of being the most scared. He couldn't perfectly recall being either. They also discussed with relish, what the next exciting instalment might be. Aengus had to brew more cocoa to see the feast through.

Their mother came in during the third batch of toast.

'I was a hero!' Paddy-last was eager to tell.

His brothers and sister quickly insisted that Paddy-last had been dreaming.

'Hush,' said their mother. 'You're making a lot of noise, you know, and Daddy has to get up for work in the morning.'

'Want some cocoa?' Aengus offered. 'There's lots of milk still, only the cream's gone.'

'I was not dreaming. You saw, too.'

'I was dreaming about maps,' said Aengus.

'Do you suppose babies dream?' Lizzie said. 'I'm sure Peter dreams he's a tiger.'

'Let me tell my dream,' Paddy-last shouted, vexed that, after making him be a hero, they were denying him its pleasures. 'I mean,' he said, 'it wasn't a dream, but real.'

'Quietly, Paddy,' his mother soothed him.

She sat down, accepting Aengus's cocoa, and borrowing a slice of Robbie's toast. Paddy-last breathlessly recounted his heroism, filling in the forgotten moments with invention. His mother had to remind him several times to keep it quiet. The older children said nothing, once they saw that their mother hadn't a notion of believing a word of Paddy's tale. They concentrated on eating, and never gave Pocket so much as a glancing thought.

In the attic, Pocket peered into the glass doorknob, humming in her green glow, her eyes wide in the darkness. Neither did she give the children much more than a glancing thought. She was the daughter of Lisgaoth, after years and years of being nothing more than a pocketful. And she was on the verge of reclaiming every inch of her lost domain.

CHAPTER 5

Parties

Naturally, the children woke late the next day, or that same day. They missed the dawn chorus, but there was enough birdsong left to sweep through the open windows in a warm and cheerful wave, when they did get up.

Lizzie awoke with a grin already on her face, and she laughed aloud, to see Paddy-last. He was practising heroic poses before the mirror.

'What's funny?' he scowled dangerously.

'You,' she said frankly, hopping out of bed. She ran to the window and was glad to see the back garden looking itself again. 'What will happen today? I hope it's as good as last night.'

'Anyhow,' said Paddy-last, 'you shouldn't have told that lie.' And he made a fierce face to the mirror.

'What lie?'

'That I only dreamed I was a hero. Mammy will think I'm still scared of silly old ghosts and stupid monsters and ignorant things like that.'

'How about Pocket?' Lizzie asked. 'Are you scared of her?'

'Are you?' Paddy asked back.

'Kind of,' Lizzie admitted. 'I'm glad she's on our side, anyhow.'

Aengus barged in, knocking as he entered. 'Oh, you're up. Hurry on, we're mounting a research party.'

'A what?'

'Research party,' Aengus repeated. 'To young Mr MacAdam, to find out how to find the rest of the door, and all that. He knows something about it, besides being a glacial deposit. So hurry on, or we won't have time before lunch.'

'Is Pocket coming?' Paddy inquired.

Aengus shrugged. 'Robbie says not, that damsels always stay behind while heroes work on their distress.'

They hurried, although Lizzie told Aengus she could take her time if she wanted to, so there. In the kitchen, they found lunch laid out for them, and their mother trying to feed a cross cousin.

'Is it lunch time?' Paddy wondered. 'Where's Daddy?'

'I'm giving you an early lunch,' said his mother, 'to match the early breakfast you had. I'll have mine with Daddy, when he comes home at one. I'm going to town with him, when he goes back to work, and you're all going to Regans' until we get back this evening. Mrs Regan is having a party for Marion's birthday.'

The four heroes groaned loudly, collapsing, rather than sitting to the table.

'You'll just have time,' their mother went on, ignoring the protest with practised ease, 'to take Peter for a walk. He's been impossible all morning.'

Peter objected to this slur, by snatching the spoon from her hand and throwing it onto the floor.

'But the Regans are all babies,' Aengus complained. 'Big babies. I wouldn't mind if they were small ones.'

'Too little for us,' agreed Paddy-last, who was a year younger than Marion. 'They always cry if you make them be villains or pack horses.'

Lizzie said, 'I don't think it's fair, for you to go around, telling people we'll go to their parties. That's all right for kids that can't think of other things to do. We can.'

'I know you can,' said her mother.

Robbie said, 'But we can't go, because we haven't a present to give Marion, have we? We'd be disgraced.'

'I'm putting two pounds into the card,' said his mother. 'Just give up the arguments, will you? You're going to Regans' and I'm going to town. For once,' she concluded with satisfaction, 'I'll get the shopping done without a circus dragging at my heels.'

Munching through their lunches, the children gave up the argument and thought instead of how selfish their mother was, and how unkind, to call them a circus.

'So what time does the old party start?' Robbie surrendered with bad grace.

'I want you here at half-past one, to get ready. Finish your lunch, and I'll fetch the pushchair. And you're not to wander too far, and come back late with feeble excuses.'

'Imagine,' said Lizzie, when her mother had left the room, 'an adventure interrupted by a birthday party.'

Paddy-last asked, 'If Mammy doesn't like us dragging at her heels, how come she always gets mad when we go off on our own to look at things?'

'You're old enough now,' said Aengus, 'not to be trying to figure out parents.'

'Come on,' Robbie said, standing to drink the last of

his milk. 'We have only an hour. We can still make MacAdams'.'

Peter was bound to his pushchair by Aengus, and they were off. As they hurried down the road, Paddy-last hoped aloud that Mrs MacAdam would be in, to give them cake. Lizzie hoped that old Mr MacAdam would be in, to tell her about the stuffed bird in the hall.

Aengus said sternly, 'You're not all going in. Young Mr MacAdam is my friend, and I don't want to frighten him off.'

'Baggit!' yelled Peter, as the wheel came off his pushchair and it tilted with a thump.

Robbie replaced the wheel, and they hurried on. Not that they really could hurry, as the wheel kept falling off, as a milk lorry crowded them off the road, and as a large blue van nearly blew them back home. But they hurried enough to feel they were hurrying, and they arrived at MacAdams' door breathless.

'You're not all going in,' Aengus said again. 'I've brought my log book, to take notes, so no-one's going to miss anything.'

Robbie thought it was time he took charge. 'Lizzie, you wait here,' he directed, 'with Peter and Paddy-last. I'm going. The research party was my idea.'

'Cheats,' said Lizzie.

'Savages,' said Paddy-last.

'Geek!' Lizzie added, and Peter echoed her noise, as a dusty-haired head popped out of Lizzie's pocket.

'I beseech you, Friend of Heroes,' said Pocket, in her lovely way, 'refrain from employing this pocket. There is so little room, although a pleasanter pocket I have never met, I do assure you.'

'But what—' began Robbie. He choked on his words, when the house door opened.

Lizzie shoved her stowaway out of sight as Mr MacAdam appeared in the doorway.

'I heard your voices,' he said. 'Come in. Come in.'

He had to repeat the invitation, as the children hesitated. But they couldn't resist the command of a maths teacher, even if they were on holidays. Young Mr MacAdam mightn't be as teacherish as his father, old Mr MacAdam, but he still was a teacher. Aengus had befriended him during an accidental meeting at the pump, and, sharing a common interest in lost civilizations, had soon forgotten his friend's professional faults. But Robbie, who liked maths, and Lizzie, who didn't, couldn't. Paddy-last simply disliked all teachers on principle.

So they shuffled in, and followed young Mr MacAdam to what he called his office, at the back of the house. Even Peter was wheeled along by a bemused Aengus. There was no sign of Mrs or old Mr MacAdam.

'Sit down,' young Mr MacAdam suggested, as they crowded into the room. 'Tell me what I can do for you. This is the famous cousin, I presume.'

Lizzie giggled, biting back, 'Dr Livingstone, to you.'

'That's him,' Aengus admitted, throwing Lizzie a killing glare.

'What we came about,' said Robbie, unwilling to waste time over common phenomena, 'is the door of Brunabawn. Aengus lost his map, and so he can't tell us, only enough to make us want to know more, and did you ever hear of a place called Lisgaoth?' He mumbled the name, nervously aware of Pocket.

'Lisgaoth?' said young Mr MacAdam, sitting down behind his desk. 'Funny, I've heard someone refer to Drumanaar by that name. Can't remember who. Mrs White, perhaps. Who mentioned Lisgaoth to you?'

'I forget,' Robbie said, trying not to look in Lizzie's direction, in case he should see the intruding Pocket.

Lizzie pinched the pocket closed, feeling the uninvited guest move within.

'As for Brunabawn,' said young Mr MacAdam, 'that is, in fact, a glacial deposit. You see, the glaciers gathered rock and soil as they moved down the country, and—' and from there he went into an explanation of glaciers, the Ice Age, and geology.

Paddy-last huddled on the floor, bored already, but trying to be the hero and survive. He didn't care how much Peter plucked him and pulled at him, he was set to endure. Being a hero, he thought, helped. But he was sure that real heroes didn't have teachers as friends.

Robbie, Aengus, and Lizzie grouped around the desk hoping to shield young Mr MacAdam from their cousin's antics. But Lizzie was forced to retreat, rather than risk his discovering the stowaway, who was getting restless.

Even when she wasn't wearing them, Lizzie's pockets were always in use, for the storage of items of scientific importance. This particular pocket, so rudely broken in upon, held various small treasures from the drainage ditch. But Pocket didn't seem to consider them of any value, as with melodious apologies, she began making herself more comfortable by tossing out the snail shells, beetles, tiny bones, and old plasters and

THE DOORKEEPERS

egg fragments. The collection hopped out, piece by piece, littering the carpet.

Peter was loudly interested. It was just the sort of game he loved, and of course he wanted to join in. Besides, he didn't agree with pushchairs indoors, or with being tied down in one, while so many lovely breakable things were just out of reach. So he abandoned the unsatisfactory Paddy-last, and began to call, 'Wow,' as he strained against his bonds. Each 'wow' was a bit louder than the 'wow' before it.

'Paddy!' Lizzie whispered angrily. She couldn't do everything.

Paddy turned his face away, to dream of buns.

'Wowowowowow!' Peter wailed.

Robbie turned a glare on Lizzie, which hint she let fall with all her castaway treasures. She was too busy trying to muffle Pocket's voice, in any case.

'The legend,' young Mr MacAdam talked on, leaving the Ice Age at last, 'is that Drumanaar possessed a bard or harper—accounts differ—which was the envy of the neighbouring clans, Torkeel most of all. Torkeel was the one to strike, attacking Drumanaar by night, and completely destroying the fort. That much of the legend is probably quite true and the original basis of the complete tale. At any rate, Drumanaar is wrecked entirely, as you will see if you visit the site.'

'Wowowowow!' yelled Peter.

'The embellishments,' said young Mr MacAdam, 'were probably invented by survivors of Drumanaar, who perhaps wanted to explain away their defeat. You had better let that child loose, you know, for he won't pipe down until he gets his way.'

81

For a moment, the listeners were confused, not knowing to whom young Mr MacAdam referred.

Then Robbie said, 'That's okay. Lizzie can take him outside.'

'Sure,' said Lizzie, willing and even eager to escape.

'Not at all,' said young Mr MacAdam. And he came around the desk, himself, to release the roaring infant.

Aengus was horrified, convinced that his friendship was heading for a disastrous end. 'He'll pull everything down,' he warned.

Young Mr MacAdam was unmoved. 'What he pulls down, we can put up again. We're used enough to babies, around here,' he said, watching Peter speed across the floor. 'I have quite a few small nieces and nephews.'

Paddy-last was astonished out of his dream of buns. 'Are you an uncle,' he gasped, amazed.

'That's the penalty,' said young Mr MacAdam, 'for having brothers and sisters. You might be an uncle yourself someday. Now, where was I?' He resumed his place behind the desk.

'If you're an uncle,' Paddy-last said, joining his brothers at the desk, 'are you only telling li—, I mean, only teasing us, or do you really mean it, about the bard and the Ice Age?'

'I beg your pardon?'

'Don't mind him,' Aengus said. 'Go on about Bruna-bawn, please, and the door. What happened to the door?'

'Yes, where is it now?' Robbie asked, to thoroughly smother Paddy-last.

'Well, Torkeel's men stole the door of Brunabawn, to

prevent Eoin Whitehand, whose palace fortress it supposedly was, from bringing aid to Drumanaar. Apparently, it was a magic door, which only opened to the full moon. That's this week, I believe,' he laughed, 'if you want to get in. One reads, too, of a key, of appointed doorkeepers, who will someday appear to restore the door. Many legends contain in their conclusion, a promise for the future. In this tale, the promise is that the door will one day be opened to emit vengeance on Torkeel, and to rescue the bard or harper, who, it seems, has been hanging around all these centuries, with no place left to go. I have something about it, somewhere.'

He crossed to a tall green filing cabinet, discouraging Peter's conversation with a trailing plant on the way. While he rooted among the files, Paddy-last furiously whispered to his brothers, that, how could they be sure young Mr MacAdam wasn't teasing, or plain lying? And Lizzie began nudging hints that she would like to edge out before Pocket could introduce herself to their 'learned friend', as Pocket insisted she would like to do.

Robbie and Aengus were too eager to pay much heed to young brother or sister. They hoped they were on the brink of adventure, and felt too much time had been wasted, between the Ice Age, and the infant cousin. Aengus opened his log book, ready to scribble down the revelations and make a quick getaway.

'Here it is. Do you want to copy it, then?' Young Mr MacAdam handed a green paper across to Aengus. 'I don't think it's much use, as an historical document, but then again, many a great explorer has successfully followed more unlikely tales. What's he doing now?' he asked of Peter.

'Wabing,' Peter admitted cheerfully, waving a tattered magazine.

Robbie went to control Peter's appetite, while Aengus feverishly wrote, with Paddy-last breathing over his shoulder. All this while, Lizzie had been awaiting the chance to make her excuses and leave. Pocket was growing louder and more insistent by the second, practically demanding the right 'to favour this sage who gives so generously of wisdom, for what is courage without knowledge?' and so on. Lizzie couldn't understand how young Mr MacAdam failed to hear Pocket's musical voice, but wanted to escape before he did. Or before she gave into the imperious demand, which was difficult to resist.

Peter, deprived of the tasty magazine, whined and mewed. Young Mr MacAdam leaned against the desk and talked of the various things he had seen babies make a meal on. He was too much of an uncle to take the infant's whine seriously, although he was more polite about it than any of Peter's own uncles would have been. After shocking Robbie with a story of a baby who had eaten a whole box of crayons, young Mr MacAdam concluded fatefully:

'I wish I had something tastier to offer him, and indeed you all. But my mother is out, and I can never tell which of her cakes are for eating, and which aren't, if you know what I mean. Are you nearly finished?' He turned to ask Aengus. And he staggered back, missing treading on Peter by inches. For of course, his wish had been granted, and only Lizzie was relieved to see the sudden tray of tea and buns: that will shut Pocket up, anyhow, she thought.

But her brothers were stunned and frightened. Would young Mr MacAdam's uncle-hood be proof against such a shock, or would the maths teacher emerge, demanding explanations?

After a moment of awful suspense, young Mr MacAdam stammered in a most unteacherlike way, 'Where . . . who . . . did . . . did I bring that in?'

'Actually,' said Lizzie, 'you did.'

'Oh. Well, then. Yes, of course. Well, then,' he said, squaring his shoulders, 'we may as well dig in, since I— since it's here.'

None of the children had any appetite for a surprise tea party. Even Paddy-last crumbled more into the carpet than into his mouth. But after giving young Mr MacAdam such a fright, the children felt they couldn't refuse. Lizzie let some lumps fall into her pocket, and tried not to unkindly wish that her wild friend would choke on them. Never had a friendship proved so difficult.

'We have to go now,' Aengus said abruptly, unable to swallow another crumb. 'Mammy's going to town, and she wants us home.'

'That's right,' Robbie said with relief. 'We'll have to run.'

Lizzie was out of the door at once, clutching her pocket closed. She was afraid young Mr MacAdam would wish they could stay. She kept running until she reached the pump, where she waited for the others.

'That's the last research party I go to,' she vowed. 'The Mad Hatter's was nothing beside it.'

'You would go in,' Robbie said. 'Anyhow, it wasn't a research party, the Hatter had.'

Paddy-last marvelled, 'He really is an uncle, though. If Daddy turned around and saw a surprise tea party, he'd tell us to put it back as quick as we got it. And Daddy won't let Peter look at a book, not to mind eat one. But it must be strange and embarrassing for kids that have a teacher for an uncle.'

'Let's just get home,' Aengus said, hurrying the three-wheeled cousin along. 'Maybe we'll have time before the next party, to assimilate the information.'

'Assimilate,' Lizzie snorted. 'I know who I'd like to assimilate right now.'

Their mother was watching out for them, to let them know they were late, and to ask, on the evidence of Peter's dirty face, where had they been eating cake? They flashed past her, giving breathless apologies to show how they had hurried, and to avoid explanations. Changing for the birthday party, Lizzie made a point of wearing a pocketless dress. There was no time to assimilate the information, or anyone else.

'Where's Pocket?' Robbie asked, as they walked up Regans' driveway.

'I hope I left her hanging in the wardrobe.'

Paddy-last remarked, 'I'm sicker of parties than I was after the p'tain. Can't we hide in the hedge until Daddy and Mammy are gone, and go home again?'

'Just the sly sort of thing you would think of,' Aengus said. 'Besides, they wouldn't be long in finding out we didn't go.'

Through Regans' front door, the reluctant guests were swept away to the playroom, where a crowd of noise was in progress. Robbie, Aengus, and Lizzie abandoned their young brother and cousin for old friends from school. Free of his critical elders, Paddy-last joined the children his own age. And Peter didn't do badly, either. He persuaded a fellow guest, who was too young to know better, to let him out of the pushchair. He then made merry by creeping about, untying shoe-laces.

The party went on as parties do, up to the entry of the official family present. This silenced everyone, and even Marion went dumb with astonishment.

At the time, Paddy-last was in the midst of various Grahams, Thompsons, and Regans, arguing whether cats or dogs were better. When the official present was wheeled in on a tea trolley, he was on the verge of proving his point forever. The squeak from his blazer pocket stopped him cold. Stuffing a hasty fist into his pocket, Paddy sidled to the back of the crowd.

No one noticed, as every eye was on the truly magnificent doll's house. Mr Regan had built it himself, from bits and pieces found in the shed, as young Louis (who had helped—or so he said) took care to announce. The house was more like a mansion. It had real doors, real stairs, carpets, and furniture, and electric lighting. There was even a tiny bell inside the luxurious hall, which Louis bragged was a genuine antique.

Recovering from shock, the guests jammed in for a closer view, with Marion protesting that they weren't to touch. Paddy was able to get right away, behind some curtains.

'What are you doing here?' he hissed into his pocket.

'The delight of Brunabawn,' Pocket said, rolling her

eyes blackly from the brown depths. 'Is laughter lost to all joy, and become an idle jest?'

'It's no joke,' Paddy said severely, encouraged to dare Pocket's authority, having her in his own pocket. 'You weren't invited. You'll get me into trouble.'

'Are you talking to yourself?' Louis Regan peeked around the curtain. 'You're crazy!'

'And you're bananas,' Paddy instantly responded. 'Go feed yourself to the gorillas.'

Louis ran off, crying out that Paddy-last was crazy, was talking to himself, and was calling Louis names. No one was interested, as Mrs Regan was directing the party to the dining-room. Even the doll's house couldn't compete with buns, orange, ice cream, and sweets.

Ordering Pocket to keep quiet, Paddy-last ran to claim his share of whatever was going. He thought he might smuggle a bun for her, and shut her up. But he kept hold of his pocket just in case. He couldn't know how useless that precaution was.

The table in the dining-room was piled high with a sickening amount of sweet things. There were two glass bowls of crisps and a basket of crackers, heaps of sweets, three plates of iced buns, and loads of biscuits. Mr Regan kept the Micky-Mouse glasses full of orange drink, and Mrs Regan dished out ice cream. Everyone grabbed. One bun, Paddy-last reasoned, wouldn't be missed. He bit into one, and let the remains drop into his pocket.

Instantly, a voice cried out, 'Mammy, that Paddy-last is stealing our buns!'

Everyone stopped grabbing, to stare, thrilled to witness a real crime.

'I'm not,' Paddy-last mumbled, burning scarlet. 'It's not for me.'

Lizzie, at the far end of the table, guessed at once what Paddy was suffering. She said, 'We promised That-Cat we'd bring her something. If you can spare it, I mean.'

'Cats don't eat buns,' Marion objected, feeling the theft deeply. They were her birthday buns.

'That-Cat does,' said Lizzie. 'Why, she eats hundreds of rats, why would she be fussy about buns?'

Mrs Regan quelled the threatening tempers, and the disappointed children went back to grabbing, eating and drinking. All except Paddy-last, who didn't dare raise his eyes in case anyone called him a cry baby. He could feel Mrs Regan watching him, and worse, he could feel the guilty bun remains in his pocket. The stowaway was gone.

When nothing was left on the table but spilled orange and pools of melted ice cream, the party was shifted to the sitting-room, where there were prizes to be won at games. Paddy-last had a vague plan of sneaking home to hide, but Mrs Regan firmly propelled him into the next room. She felt sorry for him, he looked so forlorn and unhappy, but he thought she didn't trust him out of her sight. This made him more forlorn, and made Mrs Regan sorrier, so that every time he attempted to creep away, she pounced and forced him into a game. She would have liked to get him a prize, but he proved useless at every contest. Still, Mrs Regan kept hopefully pushing Paddy into each chance, and he grew increasingly miserable.

So did Peter, underfoot. He had undone every shoelace in the room, he had chewed a hoop until an impatient competitor snatched it away, and he had whined unheeded for an hour. Giving it up at last, Peter crawled out of the room. That was a trick which never failed to bring his parents to their senses, but the party crowd hadn't even the manners to notice his escape.

Peter crept out into the hall, a bland space without any interest. He went on, until he came to a door which was ajar. Peter kneeled upright to push, and the door swung wide. He crept quietly into the playroom, and, seeing Pocket, gave a shout of delight.

'Greetings, infant child,' said Pocket, skimming down the roof of the doll's house. 'Do you, alone of all the brave band, come to my aid?' She spoke more nicely to Peter than she ever had to his cousins.

'Brafflog wassit,' Peter said. 'Plummer?'

'This smother of weary wishes and iron, is denser than I feared,' Pocket confided. 'My own magic, once so brilliant, is in dust, buried in the ancient grime of greed, chilled by an age of iron. Have you any powers, O Infant?'

'Simblog,' said Peter willingly. He headed for the house on the trolley.

He pulled himself upright by one of the wheeled legs, and did a little jig there. Standing was fun, though too much of a bother when he wanted to get somewhere. Luckily, what he had to do, now, needed standing. He began to shake the trolley, chuckling along with the murmur of rattles and creaks.

'I fear,' said Pocket, 'your endeavour is not so mighty as is your task, though you brim o'er with goodwill.'

'Dadda!' Peter began to chant with his shakings.

Pocket began to pace, one heavily booted foot floating out before the other in a wierd stride. She bent her wide-eyed gaze to the floor, muttering half-songs and snatches of tune. Each time she turned, she rolled her eyes to the ceiling and sniffed.

Peter kept chanting and shaking, until Pocket's attempted magic began producing results. The most attractive trick was the toy helicopter, which flew across the room in a suicide mission into the corner of the room. Peter left the trolley to stagger after the wonderful crash. Half-way there, he thumped down and noticed that his bright green shoes were still neatly tied. So he untied them, and having done that much, figured he might as well take them off.

The doors of the doll's house began slamming, not loudly, but enough to give Pocket pause. She stared hard, her large eyes flashing like beacons.

'Dram,' said Peter, pulling at the shoes all in vain. 'Coffing,' he grumbled, wishing they'd come off.

They did, too, and danced a jig. Then they ran fleetly away.

Peter didn't care. Running shoes off, he removed his socks in two pulls and looked around. He spied Pocket, standing rigid before the house. She was doing wonderful things.

She had summoned up enough magic to lift the laden trolley off the floor. Keeping it in the air took all her concentration.

'Wamble offbommer,' said Peter, creeping closer for a look.

'Keep your distance,' Pocket warned nervously.

The interruption let the trolley sway, turning in the

air at the same time. Peter went nearer again, and Pocket repeated her warning. The trolley swung more wildly, the doll's house slipping from side to side, shuddering as it crashed against the raised edges of the trolley top.

'Squeak!' Peter pointed. 'Wooloff dabitor!'

'I command you,' Pocket turned on him ferociously, 'meddle not!'

The instant her watch was taken off the trolley, it fell to the floor. The doll's house made a tremendous din, crashing at Peter's bare feet. He was startled into retreating right back among the helicopter.

Everyone in the party heard the fall of the doll's house. The whole party abandoned games and prizes to stampede from the sitting-room to the playroom. Once there, the smashed house astonished their wide gazes, more than it had when new and complete.

Jostling and murmuring, the party pretended to sympathize with Marion, who gaped screechlessly at the wreckage. They hadn't any doubt that Peter was to blame—they all knew what babies could do.

Peter's cousins skulked at the back of the crowd, too cowardly to claim him.

'But—,' Mrs Regan gasped. Words failed her. She couldn't believe that even a baby could pull over the heavy trolley. Yet there was no one else in the room to blame.

Then one of the guests noticed, 'There's someone hiding behind that chair.'

Hearing this, Paddy-last felt so ill, he had to run away. He missed seeing Mrs Regan bound across the room to pull a pale and trembling Louis out of hiding.

Poor Louis. While everyone was busy winning prizes, he had sneaked away to borrow his brother's helicopter. Instead, he had been the terrified witness of Pocket's house-wrecking and, worse, he had to take the blame for it.

'It wasn't me,' he protested. 'It was a dirty fairy! She was cursing and making magic, I saw her!'

The party broke up after that. All were eager to carry home the scandal of Louis's dreadful crime and shocking lies. Robbie, Aengus, and Lizzie waited only long enough to find Peter's socks under the shambles of the house. When the green running shoes couldn't be quickly located, they wrestled the protesting Peter into the pushchair, and hurried out, not even politely pausing to thank Mrs Regan for the good time they had had. There was no point in thanking Marion, who had found her voice and stood in the middle of the late present, using it.

'Dirty fairy?' said Robbie.

'Pocket strikes again,' said Aengus.

Lizzie worried, 'I hope Mammy doesn't blame us for going home early. She told us to wait at Regans' until six.'

They found Paddy-last swinging on their own front gate. He said, 'I thought you'd never come. Did they arrest Pocket?'

'No,' said Robbie. 'When did she ever take the blame for her crimes? Let that phenomenon loose, will you,' he told Aengus. 'I can't hear myself think.'

Aengus said, 'Let him loose yourself. Am I my cousin's keeper, or something?'

'It was an awful thing for her to do,' Lizzie said,

reluctantly, 'though she is my friend. She hasn't been herself ever since she got the Historic Doorknob. Where is she now, Padders?'

Paddy-last shrugged, saying he was fed up with her.

Robbie, in exasperation, knelt to untie the infant. He reeled back with a shout, and more noticeably, Peter stopped crying, when Pocket's head suddenly appeared from the tiny pocket on the bib of the baby's suit. The children watched with wonder as she struggled out of the impossibly small space, but once she had wriggled free, they got mad, for in one starved hand, she held the little bell from the hall of the doll's house. Even Pocket's queenly bearing could not quench their righteous anger.

'I hope,' Robbie said coldly, 'you have a good explanation for your house-wrecking and your stealing.'

CHAPTER 6

After the Parties

'Stealing?' Pocket repeated grandly.

Robbie, every bit as grand, said, 'I don't suppose you're only taking the loan of that bell? Of course, you couldn't ask us to get the bell for you, legally. That's not what we're for. We're just pockets to you, pockets for you to creep into as soon as our backs are turned.'

'I am the daughter of Lisgaoth,' said Pocket. 'I need not answer to you, nor to any of your kind.'

'Don't, then,' said Robbie. 'I don't think I'd much like your answers, anyhow. Next time a distressed damsel asks me for help, I'm going to make sure she's bound and gagged and locked in an ivory tower, before I even blow the dust of Sword Lightstriker. Goodbye, and I hope I find you've got lost when I come home.'

In a temper, he grabbed the pushchair and pushed it, with Peter, out of the gate. 'Who wants a chariot race?' he furiously invited his brothers and sister.

'I do!' Paddy-last accepted. 'I'll get the wheelbarrow.' He ran off around the house.

There was an uncomfortable and hot silence. Robbie fumed in the road. Pocket stood frozen with cold anger. Lizzie and Aengus exchanged doubtful glances. As the trundle of the barrow sounded, Lizzie whispered to

Aengus, 'You go. You might do something with Robbie, and I'll see what I can do about my wild friend.'

'Okay,' Aengus said. 'But you'd better make her realize she can't treat us like this.'

Paddy-last arrived with the barrow. He climbed in, and Aengus took up the reins. Lizzie gave the word and they were off.

The race went at a furious pace, and helped Robbie work off a lot of his vexation. The barrow's weight gave it a great speed, once it was under way. At the fork of the road, the pushchariot cast its loose wheel. Robbie caught it and gave it to Peter to hold. Peter kept throwing it overboard, and, as the thundering wheelbarrow took the lead, Robbie abandoned the cast wheel. The road inclined slightly, giving the lighter pushchariot an advantage. They flew along neck to neck, until they came to Grahams' gate. There, Paddy-last flung himself overboard. He was sick.

'Well, we would have won,' Aengus panted. He sat down to rest in his chariot.

'If you'd come in first, you mean,' said Robbie. 'I feel better now. Nothing like a chariot race. We should have had one yesterday, instead of letting Pocket talk us into trouble. Okay, Padders?'

'Maybe Mrs Graham will give me a drink of orange,' Paddy-last said. 'Even cake. I wouldn't mind cake, while Pocket's not around.'

'Check your pockets first,' Robbie advised.

Aengus could see that Robbie, though in better humour, wasn't ready to reconsider the adventure. He said,

'There's James.'

The oldest of the Graham sons appeared from behind the house. He was liberally splattered with paint, and carried a pail of brushes. Seeing the children, James left the pail on the doorstep and approached.

'Hello,' he said, stepping clear over the gate, to the admiration of his visitors. 'If you're looking for the kids, they're gone to the village. I packed them off, so's I could get some work done here.'

'We're just having a chariot race,' Robbie said. 'Did they tell you about Marion's doll's house?'

'Surely, and Louis's poor lying. Is this the famous cousin?' He got down to Peter's level. 'You didn't waste time breaking his pushchair.' He tickled the infant and got a punch in the nose. 'Teaching him your tricks, too.'

'That's one of his own tricks,' Paddy-last said. 'Can't teach a new kid old tricks, you know.'

'No, I didn't know,' said James. 'You have the barrow along, too, I see. You might give me the loan of it. Badger's new gate is around the back. It would save me bother if I got it over to him now.'

'Sure,' Aengus agreed instantly. 'What's he doing with the old one?' He was always on the alert for building materials.

James said, 'I hope he burns it.'

He wheeled the barrow around the house, and all but Peter helped load the new gate. It was a fine one, all curls and bars.

'Different from the old one,' Paddy-last shrewdly noticed. 'Did that one break?'

'The old one is the curse of the crossroads, so it is,' said James, as they all headed for Joyces'. 'I'll never forget the day, long ago, when I had to bring a letter to

Miss Joyce, one that the postman left with us by mistake. The blessed gate wouldn't open, however much I kicked at it, until herself came flying out to ask me what I was at. The spiteful thing opened then. But it closed fast enough when I tried to make my getaway. Caught the tail of my coat, and I'd be there yet, if Badger hadn't come along.'

'We had a doorknob like that,' Paddy-last said. 'It broke a window.'

'But Badger won't burn the old gate, will he?' Aengus asked. 'He might let us have it, if he doesn't want it.'

'What for?' Robbie wondered. 'We have enough things like it.' And then he fell silent, struck by an idea.

Aengus said, 'I need an observation post. And we have to have something to do, if we're not going to do anything else.'

Paddy-last said, 'Build me a retreat like Lizzie's. You promised you would, before I accidently burned the River Nile's map. Remember?'

'Well,' said James, 'you can ask Badger, anyhow. He can't do worse than say no.'

They arrived at Joyces'. The children discreetly retired to the far side of the road, as Miss Joyce and Badger came out of the house. Miss Joyce was not fond of children, especially if she suspected them of having designs on her gate.

She and Badger were happy to see the new gate, and after a lot of kind words, they persuaded James to hang it at once. The loops were ready to swing on the new, and the only work involved was in taking down the old one. It didn't seem to want to go.

Amid splinters and awkward nails, Badger recalled

aloud the day his grandfather had built the old gate, putting together bits and pieces, 'every one of them contrary', that had collected in the shed. It was rather a nice looking gate, of wood with a rounded top, a rusty bolt, and three impossibly long hinges which were almost invisible beneath many coats of paint. Those hinges were as famous for their piercing shriek as the gate itself was for its spiteful behaviour.

Aengus longed to call it all his own, but Robbie, listening attentively to Badger's stories, decided that some part of it was kin to the Historic Doorknob and the bell from Marion's doll's house. He so liked the idea of having found part of the missing door without Pocket, that he forgave her all her faults, and prepared to adventure again.

The old gate finally surrendered. It came away suddenly, to bang Badger's shins. They leaned it against the garden wall, and it slid down to crack James in the ankle.

The new gate behaved properly, however. It fairly leapt into place and swung there without a murmur.

'We'll have to get a dog for sure,' Badger said, 'or how will we know when someone's coming?'

'About time, too,' said his sister. 'Leave the old gate around the back, now. Would you like tea?' she asked James.

'No, thanks. I have to get back to the painting.' He looked at the children.

'We're not going yet,' said Aengus. 'We have to ask Badger something.'

James left them.

Miss Joyce waited around for a while, nagging Badger

to leave the old gate in the shed before he began telling his lies to the children. Badger kept agreeing until she went away into the house.

'So what do you want to know?' he asked, leaning comfortably over the new gate.

'Do you need that old gate for anything?' Aengus asked. 'I could use it, if you don't want it.'

'I don't want it,' Badger snorted. 'Sure, you can have it. It will be company for the fairy,' he added, laughing.

'It's not funny,' Robbie said. 'Why are you always laughing about magic? It's serious, and dangerous.'

Badger roared with laughter. 'You sound like Mary,' he said, meaning his sister. 'You'll never get sense.'

'Come on,' Aengus said to Robbie. 'Let's get this home.'

'No, really,' Robbie insisted, to Badger. 'Do you know what magic is really like?'

'Come inside and talk to herself,' Badger invited, still laughing. 'She'll tell you all you want, and more, and never another night will you sleep easy in your beds. Or anywhere. You'll be seeing the grey hoards of Torkeel around every corner.'

Bellowing with amusement, Badger left them with the old gate.

'What's he mean?' Paddy-last asked.

'If it's what I think,' said Robbie, 'we'd better get this gate home.'

They loaded the gate onto the wheelbarrow and turned homewards. Paddy-last took charge of Peter, as both Aengus and Robbie had to manage the gate. It was as contrary in the barrow as ever it had been hanging, and from the crossroads all the way home, kept them busy and bruised. If it wasn't sliding off, it was tilting the barrow over; when it wasn't hitting them in the shins, it was jabbing their hands with splinters. Aengus was afraid Robbie would want to ditch it, and kept babbling about building observation posts. Finally Robbie said,

'If I thought it was only for building, I wouldn't be bothered. You'll see. We're going to fling this gate in Pocket's dirty fairy face.'

'Oh, brilliant!' said Paddy-last with complete approval.

Aengus said nothing. He hoped Lizzie was having better success with Pocket, or they'd have to give up their adventure entirely.

They turned into their own road, and had home in sight, when Lizzie met them shouting. She was greatly excited. All they could understand was, 'She can, she really can do magic!'

*   *   *

After the boys had raced off, and Lizzie had had Pocket all to herself, she had said, 'Are you satisfied now?'

Pocket's sharp pasty face distorted with emotion and her eyes flashed dreadfully. 'You are as great a peril yourselves,' she gulped, 'as were all the p'tain of Torkeel.'

'It's your own fault,' Lizzie shrugged. 'We wanted to rescue you and all that, but how can we, when you want to do it all yourself? Robbie says that distressed damsels always wait out of the way, while the bold knights go off to slay the foe. And Robbie would know.

He's the magic adventure expert on the panel. Do you think I need adventure to keep me busy? I could be tracking stoats and badgers. Aengus would rather be at his maps, and Paddy-last never had any time for adventure, even when he had the time to spare.

'But last month, when we heard that Peter was going to be plonked on us, to lay waste our summer holidays, Robbie had the idea of getting an adventure before we got a cousin, so that we'd have something nice to remember when summer was gone. It's Robbie that talked the rest of us into ransacking the neighbourhood for adventure. We didn't find it, of course, but it's Robbie's talk that had us ready when it found us.

'And now you sneer and fiddle us out of the daring deeds we were looking forward to, and now you've got Robbie against you. If Robbie decides not to bother with you, so will we all.'

Pocket smoothed some of the wrinkles from her face with a strand of filthy satin. Lizzie's flow of reason made Pocket patiently stubborn, if not sorry for having insulted the heroic Robbie.

'And yet,' she said, 'does he, this magic expert, not see why I must recall the door, and yet cannot myself open it?'

'No, we don't,' Lizzie said. 'You don't explain anything, do you? And you don't be very polite about not explaining, either.'

For a moment, she thought Pocket was again going to draw herself up into the haughty daughter of Lisgaoth. Instead, the face creased pathetically.

'Yet the magic is of your own,' Pocket said. 'A spell laid down by mortal muddling: I call upon the door, which assembled, the appointed doorkeepers open. By that clumsy ruse, is Brunabawn protected from my grey work in wishing, from my long abode in the iron-bound homes of men. Do you understand, do you see?'

'Sort of. I mean, I know about iron being deadly to your kind of people, from Paddy. I don't see how all that rigmarole's going to help, though. I mean, the door itself must be pretty iron-sick by now, mustn't it?'

'I might cleanse it with song,' said Pocket. 'My own state, I may deal with, when our task is done.'

'Song,' said Lizzie.

'Yes, for song is my power; was my power. Ah, could you but see my true magic! I scrabble at a darkened pane, blinded and unrevealed to those who would look in. You catch some faint hum of former wealth, and wonder that it suffices not. I see but dimly into your minds, and mourn your lack.'

Lizzie stared at the huddle of grimy silk and dusty hair, at the pale, pinched face and spidery limbs.

'So all your magic is just songs?'

'Just songs!' Pocket exclaimed, indignant. 'Hear then, a faint whim of former power, and judge what once I held.' In a low voice, Pocket began to sing:

'The rath is empty on the hill,
The fort below is closed and still.
Lisgaoth is gone like drifting smoke,
Rising, bending, blowing, broke.
The ivory daughter is buried deep,
In Pocket all the white songs sleep.'

As she held the last note of the unbearably mournful tune, Lizzie saw the magic. That is, she could suddenly imagine in perfect detail, what Lisgaoth had been, and knew from that, how entirely empty Drumanaar now was. And Brunabawn became in Lizzie's mind, the entrance way to a ringing palace of radiant lights, peopled with glowing warriors whose chief, Eoin Whitehand, was the betrothed of the silver-haired, the emerald-eyed, the ivory daughter of Lisgaoth.

Although Lizzie still saw with her own eyes, the familiar front garden, and the weird Pocket, the song so overpowered her, that she became blind to all but its visions. Until that last note faded, she couldn't stir. When it did finally die away into a faint vibration, she jumped to her feet.

'Wait there,' she told Pocket. 'I'll fetch the others. You'll have to show them.'

She dashed up the road, calling. The boys came at once, dumping the barrow and gate by the roadside. They reached their own gate just as their parents pulled up in the car.

'Get that wheelbarrow back where it belongs,' said their father, before he was even out of the car.

As Aengus turned to obey, their mother asked, 'Why are you home so early?'

Lizzie began to answer, when their father said, 'And you've broken the pushchair, I see. Where's the wheel?'

Robbie ran to find the forgotten wheel, and didn't hear his mother ask, 'What have you done with Peter's shoes?'

'I'll find them,' Paddy-last volunteered, to get out of the way quickly.

Lizzie was left to make excuses. She made plain their own innocence, in the affair of the wrecked house, but nobly refrained from blaming Louis. There was no point in blaming Pocket.

'I think there's a jinx on this neighbourhood,' her father said, as they went into the house. 'Thompson's clothes line disappears and reappears, Faller's shop is raided of sweets, that return the next morning, and now Marion's doll's house.'

Lizzie, alarmed by this information, ran off. She muttered that she would help Paddy find the green running shoes, but, going in the wrong direction, she met Aengus instead. He was struggling all alone, with Badger's gate.

'Give me a couple of hands,' Aengus said, as soon as he saw her. 'This thing's alive.'

'Listen,' Lizzie said, seizing the wheelbarrow so wildly that it overturned, 'those chocolates we wished for were robbed from the village, and now they're back where they came from.'

'I forgot,' Aengus said. 'They're bottle caps now.' He explained how he had made this discovery, and how he had forgotten about it afterwards in the excitement of Pocket. 'I expect Paddy-last wished for them,' he said. 'There's millions of them.'

'They're probably robbed, as well,' Lizzie said. 'It seems to me we're bound to get arrested, going or coming. I hope you talked Robbie back into this lark. If he doesn't like helping Pocket, he'll have to like helping us.'

'Give me a hand with this, anyhow,' Aengus said.

'But did you talk him round?' Lizzie insisted, as she helped drag the gate on to the barrow. 'Maybe the notes young Mr MacAdam gave you will help. It's too bad you missed seeing Pocket's magic. Robbie would have liked that.'

As they manhandled gate and barrow, Lizzie tried to describe the effects of Pocket's music. She was not very successful. Aengus's mind was full of those notes, for he knew that if Robbie wanted a good excuse for casting adventure into the outer darknesses, the notes would provide one.

The barrow stuck fast in their own front gate, and they began quarrelling how to get it through. Robbie returned with Peter's wheel, then, and after ordering them aside, roughly shoved the barrow forward.

'We'll put it in the back, where we can keep an eye on it,' he said. 'After tea, when we assimilate your information from young Mr MacAdam, I'll tell you what I think about this old gate. We'll plan an action, then, and lay down the law to Pocket.'

So they heaved and hauled their burden, and by what seemed a miracle, got the old gate and the wheelbarrow into the back garden.

'Now, where's Paddy-last?' Robbie asked.

'Here I am,' Paddy-last said. He crept over the end wall of the garden. He had been hiding in Lizzie's Hermit's Retreat, on the other side. 'I was looking for Peter's running shoes.'

'Running shoes!' Robbie said scornfully. 'The kid can hardly walk, never mind run. Listen, Paddy, we're having an important meeting after tea, and you're not to slide out of it. We're going to finish this thing and show Pocket what business means.'

'Well,' Paddy-last said, 'I have to write out a song first.'

'You have not,' Aengus said.

'I have so. I'll forget it if I don't.'

'There's no fear,' Lizzie said, 'of you ever forgetting any of your old songs.'

'Too bad if there was,' Robbie said, all bustle. 'Getting rid of Pocket is more important. Do you think Torkeel's gang is going to stand by forever? Once they find out what we did to the p'tain, they'll get after us, as well as Pocket.'

On this frightening reminder, they went in for their tea. Robbie shouldn't have mentioned Torkeel, how-ever. Paddy-last had no great liking for Pocket, and the threat of Torkeel appealed less. All through tea, he considered heroism in his cowardly way. The dangers of being a mere friend or relative seemed less. After all, some friends and relatives must survive, or how could a hero live happily ever after? Besides, someone ought to stay behind to mind the house.

So, when tea was eaten and washed up, Paddy-last repeated his intention of writing down his new song.

His brothers and sister were furious, but Paddy-last had a powerful ally.

'Leave poor Paddy alone,' their mother said.

'We only want him for a game,' Robbie told her. 'We need him. It's not fair: when we don't need him, you make us take him along, and now you won't let us.'

'Leave him alone,' their mother repeated. 'You never need him when he needs you.'

Fuming, the three retreated.

'Little coward,' Lizzie said. 'And he told me this morning he wasn't afraid of monsters or ghosts.'

Robbie said, 'Never mind him, for now. Let's get at your log book, Aengus.'

Aengus fetched the log book, and, when Robbie said that no one could read such writing but the designer, he read aloud:

'The warmth of unstinted courage shall protect the brilliance within, lest years of iron-bound toil threaten and darken those beaming blossoms. For mortal good-wishing forever undoes the chains of mortal ill-wishes. Look to the doorkeepers, who announce themselves:

> *'For one who knows the names of way*
> *The opening star will turn.*
> *From one who puts the words to song,*
> *The silver hinges learn.*
> *To one who welcomes all as friend,*
> *The ringing joy discerns.*
> *With these without the moonlit door,*
> *Within the bright key burns.'*

Aengus paused here, waiting for Robbie to see the blank in their ranks.

'Is that all?' Robbie asked.

'No. It says: "*She alone shall gather, she alone shall guide, until all Brunabawn is roused and Torkeel vanquished. Thus spells the speller Joyce, who in peril recovered and concealed the parts, the peace of the hills, to restore, confirm, and seal.*" '

'Won't be much peace, once Eoin Whitehand gets after Torkeel,' Robbie remarked. 'Go on. That can't be all.'

'See for yourself,' Aengus said, passing over the book. 'There's nothing to it, really, if Torkeel leave us alone.'

While Robbie complained in mutters about the hand-writing, Aengus and Lizzie looked at each other: what would happen now? they silently questioned. For there was no place for Robbie among the assembly instructions for the door.

Robbie saw that for himself, straightaway, but he didn't want to admit it. 'Aengus is the mapmaker, so he knows the names of way, or any young Mr MacAdam taught him. Lizzie's the wild friend of all, and Paddy-last never shuts up putting words in songs. The key's inside. Where do I get off, or on, or in on this? It's a cinch, they only want the hinges, and it's an open and shut case, if Torkeel leave them alone. If they don't—' Robbie looked up from his mutterings and said, 'It's obvious. The swordbearer, the handiest hero of all, is left out because you need an armed escort. We can't all have our hands full of doorknobs, bells, and hinges.'

'Great!' Aengus and Lizzie shouted with relief.

Aengus added, 'Young Mr MacAdam said the door opens at full moon. That's tomorrow night,'—he knew, that being the sort of thing Great Explorers had to know—'so unless we want Pocket hanging around for another month, we'll have to act fast. I'm sure Torkeel won't wait idle for another month.'

'Don't worry about Torkeel,' Robbie said. He took up Sword Lightstriker. 'I'll fix them. There won't be much for old Eoin Whitehand to—'

Something short of an explosion rocked the house, before Robbie could finish his sentence. It seemed to come from the back garden.

The children could hear their parents rushing out, below, and the wail of a terrified infant arose from

Lizzie's room, where Peter was in bed. They ran to a window to look out.

'Nothing,' their father was saying, 'except this.'

They saw him cross the lawn to take up the torn and twisted old gate. It was violently wrenched apart, and showed pale streaks of paintlessness.

'The hinges,' Robbie choked, furious with himself for not having brought them indoors. 'I knew it. I guessed directly. Those hinges belong to Brunabawn.'

'But who's taken them now?' Aengus asked. 'Pocket or Torkeel?'

Pocket spoke up from behind, 'Torkeel, I fear. Empowered by twilight, Torkeel has made a bold attack. When mankind delays to talk, the hidden people do not hesitate to act.'

They whirled around, to see her wringing her hands and accusing them with her huge eyes. A shadow of defeat overcast her pale face. Was she to be left out in the world of iron forever, or worse, finally and forever fall captive to Torkeel?

Robbie said with relish, 'Well, then, we'll just have to attack back.' He waved Sword Lightstriker, and Pocket shrank back. 'Are you coming?' he asked the others. 'You needn't, if you don't like. You're only door-keepers.'

'But Torkeel is miles away,' Aengus objected.

'We'd never catch up,' said Lizzie.

'Not if we stand here, jawing,' Robbie said. 'Come on. It's not quite dark yet.'

As they rushed out, Paddy-last poked his head from behind the sitting-room door, to ask where they were going. He was told to mind his own business, which he thought he could best do by following. When he was in any danger of being left out, Paddy-last forgot the dangers of being let in.

There were a good few beams of fading sunlight left, as the children went hotfoot down the road. Robbie led, having a vague plan of going around by MacAdams', along the main road, and completing the circle by turning for home at the crossroads. He was sure that the thieves, however cunningly magic, could not pass through a summer's evening without leaving a trace.

At the well opposite the ruined cottages, the children met Mr Thompson, walking a fleet of greyhounds, and they panted to a halt.

Robbie asked, 'Have you seen anyone strange pass?'

'Funny you should ask that,' Mr Thompson said, reining in the hounds. 'A small black-coated fella took off past our house, not long back. I wouldn't have noticed, but he set the dogs howling. What's up?'

Without answering, Robbie, Aengus, and Lizzie ran on. Paddy-last paused only long enough to inquire, 'Did he look dangerous?' and he didn't even wait for a reply, as he didn't like to see his brothers and sister getting ahead so quickly. If he was going to be in with them, Paddy-last wanted to make the most of the safety in numbers. He ran to keep up with them.

They hastened past the road to Torkeel, under the shadow of Drumanaar, and wavered to a halt at the path leading up into the meadows on the hill.

'Anyone pass?' Robbie gasped out to Badger, who was coming onto the road there.

'Not that I saw,' said Badger. 'What style of an anyone?'

111

'Black coat,' Lizzie panted, 'and small.'

Badger shook his head. 'Ask the sister,' he advised. 'She's feeding the calves above Connicker.' He passed on.

'Connicker?' said Robbie.

'That meadow,' Aengus said. 'She'll be in the next.'

'What's up, anyhow,' Paddy-last wheezed.

They turned into the path. On either side were the stone walls that divided the land, and a heavy sweep of bramble, hawthorn, and rank weeds. The grass underfoot deadened the noise of their passage, as the barriers along the way damped the dying sun. Their steps slowed as the ground sloped upwards, and the eerie atmosphere of the hedgerow pressed them down.

'I don't like it,' Paddy-last whined to himself, wishing in vain that Lizzie would lend him a comforting hand.

None of them liked it, for at the best of times this sour-scented path was oppressive. It was too secretive, too private, and always shaded by the unchecked hedges that narrowed the way to a single file. Anything could jump out from anywhere, to crowd them into the brambles if not worse.

As they passed through the deepest shade, where trees in the field beyond cast black shadows, their steps wavered. They could hear Miss Joyce soothing the calves ahead, a comforting sound despite her dislike of children. Once they reached her, they could go into the wonderfully open meadow.

Suddenly they heard her shout, 'What are you at!' followed by a clanging thump.

Paddy-last hung back, Aengus and Lizzie hesitated, but Robbie said, 'She can't mean us,' and hurried them on.

By the calf-crowded gate, they found Miss Joyce picking up a bucket, and sourily regarding a prone black figure. She looked up as the children approached.

'Is this some wicked game?' she scolded. 'Haven't you been told to keep away from farm animals?'

'We're chasing him,' Robbie explained. 'He stole something of ours.'

'It isn't a game,' Lizzie promised. 'It's serious.'

Aengus wondered, 'Can we touch him?'

They gathered around the huddle of rusty black. He was small and hunched, with a black hat pulled so far down that only a white beak of a nose could be seen. Miss Joyce nudged the still form with her foot. A faint sigh ruffled the air.

'Who is he?' she asked. 'You should have called the police.'

'Yes, we should,' Paddy agreed. 'Let's do it now.'

'I think he's from Torkeel,' Robbie said. 'I'll search him.'

He bent, reaching for the black coat with a trembling reluctance. The presence of Miss Joyce was encouraging, for surely nothing magic would happen before the sensible eyes of a grown-up. But as soon as Robbie came within a breath of touching, the figure sprang into life.

Robbie whipped out his sword, and Miss Joyce lifted the bucket. Aengus held his ground, while Lizzie fell flat on her back, knocking Paddy into the hedge.

The little black bundle bounced in their midst, insanely giggling. He didn't seem at all abashed by his surrounding foes.

Robbie swung his sword, and the little man jumped.

He swung again, and the little man ducked. Up and down, the hunched black-coated bundle jumped, laughing and, apparently, in no hurry to escape while he could enjoy teasing his assailants. Aengus, Lizzie, and Paddy-last were unarmed and helpless to do anything. Robbie kept trying, but it was Miss Joyce who put the lid on things, or rather, the bucket: she clapped it over the bouncing hatted head, and Robbie's sword fell, thwack! on the stilled target.

A great cloud of dust arose as Sword Lightstriker struck, making the four children and Miss Joyce fall back coughing. A piercing 'Eeeee!' whistled up to the invisible sky.

Through the cloud, Miss Joyce called, 'Run!'

'No,' Robbie said, choking on the dust. 'The hinges.'

He surged blindly forward, feeling the ground with one hand and waving Sword Lightstriker with the other. He found the bucket, upside down on the grass, and knocking it over, found what felt like the hinges.

'I've got them,' he shouted, choking again.

They ran down the hill, blundering into brambles and each other until the end of the path shone brightly ahead. The cloud of dust seemed to follow them all the way, squeezing the air and the evening sun into a breathless grey. But on the road, all was plain, was strangely ordinary in the summer twilight.

Miss Joyce coughed, when the children would stop to catch clean breaths. 'Quickly, our house is nearest. Quickly!' she grabbed at them, pushing them on.

They hurried on. From the grey clouded path, they now heard a thunder of many feet, a clash of weapons, and the dreadful baying of hounds.

Of course, Torkeel's chieftain and all his band must have awaited the thief at some point, or had been coming to meet him. Such a vital mission could not go unguarded, and only the lingering wakefulness of the countryside had prevented the hoards from descending in force, earlier.

But caution seemed thrown to the winds now, as the thunder pursued the children onto the road. Robbie glanced back once, and was more frightened to see nothing than he would have been to see the deadliest foe.

Miss Joyce pressed on. 'Through our gate, and straight into the house,' she directed.

Here was the new gate, the path, and the front door opened by a bewildered Badger. He was bowled over by the five fugitives.

The sudden entrance was so puzzling, Badger couldn't think what questions to ask. He stood gaping, as his sister slammed and bolted the door, and with the children, peeked out of the window. They saw nothing but the oncoming night.

'Gosh, it must be late,' Robbie suddenly realized. And looking around the dim, snug room, he spied the clock. 'Half-ten!'

'We'll be killed,' Paddy-last solemnly declared.

Which made Robbie, Aengus, Lizzie, and Miss Joyce burst out laughing.

'What's up?' Badger dug out a question to ask.

'Nothing that concerns you,' his sister said. 'I want you to fetch their father. Tell him to bring the car, they aren't fit to walk home. And you had better go through the back way,' she added, peering out, 'across the fields until you get to Cranslee Road. Go on.'

Shaking a bewildered head, Badger went.

'Well done,' Lizzie said, full of admiration at this forceful handling of a brother.

'Sit down,' Miss Joyce said. 'I could do with a cup of tea after all that.'

The children sat down, two each on the hobs at either side of the open fire. Joyces' cottage was an old-fashioned but cosy house, with kitchen, dining-room, and living-room combined into one. The clean-swept floor was of bare cement, the walls were brown-papered, and the ceiling a smoky white. The only decoration was a collection of calendars, of which there were four with four different pictures: a basket of kittens, a hurling team, a field of cows, and a pair of budgies.

'Switch on the light,' Miss Joyce commanded, as she wet the tea. 'It's by the door, there.'

Aengus obeyed. The others preferred the firelit quiet, but he wanted to more closely observe this lost civilization they had found shelter in. It was almost another world to him.

'That child's falling asleep,' Miss Joyce said of Paddy-last. 'Better leave him so. We'll just move him to the couch, so he won't fall into the fire and put it out.'

Robbie and Aengus between them, shifted Paddy-last to the shiny blue couch. Then, with Miss Joyce and Lizzie, they sat to the table and indulged in mugs of tea and fatly buttered slices of madeira cake.

The children didn't say anything, as they tried not to feel too self-conscious about the crumbs that fell to the floor. They were waiting for their hostess to ask questions, as they were wondering at how ably she had aided their flight. But Miss Joyce said nothing, except to press more cake on them, to refill their mugs, and to remark how she was enjoying her tea.

'I'll parcel some cake for the young lad,' she said, when they had eaten their fill. 'Your father should be here soon.' She began clearing the table, refusing the children's offer of help. 'Just sit still,' she told them 'and take your rest.'

So they did, uneasily, as she washed up in a plastic basin on the table.

The silence would have been friendly, if the children hadn't been so curious about Miss Joyce. Between staring at the different calendars, they watched her, trying to guess what she was thinking.

Sitting down with them by the fire, she said, 'I expect Badger's having tea, now, with your parents' knowing you're all right.'

Robbie simply had to ask, 'Aren't you wondering—'

'No,' said Miss Joyce, abruptly cutting in. 'Of all the children that ever were, you lot must be the worst for meddling. Rousing the hills, as you're doing, it's too late for any wondering.'

'It wasn't us!' Lizzie exclaimed. She was hurt by the very idea. 'We're trying to un-rouse them, after all the meddling the Maddens did, and they weren't children, were they?'

They stared at Miss Joyce, and she stared back. There was a long silence.

Finally, Robbie said, with careful politeness, 'We're sorry to have upset you and all, but we couldn't help it, really we couldn't. It will be all finished by tomorrow. At least, I hope so. We want to get rid of the trouble as much as you could. More, maybe, because she is right in our house. This is the only way we can do it.'

'Hmph,' said Miss Joyce, or something like that. 'I'm sure you do, now you've begun and can see what you've let yourselves in for.'

'But we didn't,' Lizzie protested. 'It's not our fault at all.'

Aengus nudged her. He asked in a careless manner, 'By the way, was that Speller Joyce some relation of yours?'

'Some relation,' Miss Joyce laughed shortly. 'I wouldn't have minded those ridiculous hinges if he hadn't been. "The peace of the hills hangs by them", so we were always told, but Badger never heeded, or I'd be minding those hinges still.' She threw a sod of turf onto the fire, and belaboured the embers angrily with the poker. Sparks flew up the vast chimney.

'They don't mix,' she went on, 'mortal folk and fey, not in their work, their play, or their magic. Old Speller Joyce was an old fool, as you're young fools. He would have it, that the good of his own people depended on the good of the hidden ones, although it's scarce consideration they ever gave us. Pure ridiculous—the best good is to keep your distance. He had to meddle, had to fret his days away in worry over some silly creature that escaped the fate she deserved, along with the rest of her kind up the way. Never did him an ounce of good, nor any of us, for all the care we gave those hinges like they were gold. I don't like it, I don't want to hear about it, and it's a pity, so it is, that you were never taught to mind your business.' She pounded furiously at the fire, too angry to say any more.

118

They all watched the glowing uprush of heat.

Robbie thought: *so she believes in magic; I wonder if I always will, no matter how old I get.*

Aengus thought: *if she knew that much, why didn't she try to find out more; I would have.*

Lizzie brooded on the unreasonableness of grown-ups, on their illogical behaviour. She thought: *why did she give us all cake and tea if she's so mad at us? I wouldn't have.*

Miss Joyce eventually gave voice once more, saying, 'Well, I suppose I'll have to wish you luck, if you really mean to do all you say. I hope you don't regret it, that's all. You've stirred the pot, now mind it doesn't boil over.'

They all waited, after that, in uneasy truce. The clock ticked noisily, the fire hissed, and for a long, long while, both children and Miss Joyce thought they would never hear anything else.

At last came the sound they had all been longing for, the familiar drone of the car. Robbie jumped up, Aengus gabbled out a hasty, 'Thanks for the cake,' and Lizzie dragged Paddy-last to the door.

'Don't mention it,' Miss Joyce called after them, as delighted to see them go, as they were to be gone.

CHAPTER 7

Kidnapped

In order to satisfy his father, and to get them home to bed without hassle, Robbie told an abstract and vague tale of being frightened on the hillside, of having to soothe Paddy-last at Joyces'. They were all extremely tired, and longed for nothing more adventurous than sleep.

But the next morning was different. It was the dawn of what they hoped was the final day.

Paddy-last was the first to waken, and his eyes opened on the share of cake Miss Joyce had parcelled for him. Lizzie had kindly left it by his pillow, and he mistook it for a dream come true. He ate it at once, pursuing the crumbs down among the bedclothes and stirring up a crosspatch.

'You savage,' Lizzie kicked out. 'Now we'll be all crumbs until Mammy does the sheets.'

'Won't,' Paddy-last said. 'I've found them all. Where did it come from? Do you think I could have been wishing in my dreams, on account of all that cake I didn't get yesterday, like a feast of famine?'

'No. It's because you fell asleep at Joyces' and missed everything. Peter's more a comrade in arms than you are.' She proceeded to fill him in on everything, from Pocket's magic, to the chocolate raid, the log book, and the hinges, with all Miss Joyce had said concerning them.

After it was all told, Paddy-last said, 'Were you ever scared?'

'Scared,' Lizzie said, considering. It was difficult to think of being scared with a full day of sunlight just beginning, with her mother singing at the top of her voice, with knowing all was well and safe at home. 'The scaredest I ever was,' she said at last, 'was the time I broke Uncle Fergus's binoculars.'

Paddy-last made a restless movement. 'He couldn't kill you,' he said. 'I wouldn't be scared of an uncle.'

'Sure, big hero,' said Lizzie. 'We all know you're not scared of any*one*, just scared of every*thing*.'

'Makes sense,' Paddy-last said. 'People can't be as scary even when you break their binoculars. They can't really hurt you, like dark sorts of things can.'

'Why don't you make up your mind whether you're going to be a hero or not?'

'And he didn't kill you, after all,' Paddy-last went on. 'He only called you names. That's no adventure.'

'Suit yourself,' Lizzie said. 'Just make up your mind, if you have one.' She rolled out of bed, and went to the cot. 'Rise and shine, Peter pumpkin,' she called, rattling the bars. 'Wake up, wild friend of mine.'

Peter rose and shone, popping up like a tropical sun. He began a conversation, and Lizzie pretended to join in, not to annoy Paddy-last, but to encourage Peter.

Paddy-last was annoyed, though. He rolled over and sang into his pillow, to show he didn't care.

Aengus walked in. 'Are you going to get up or not?' he asked. 'Pocket wants us in the garden. Hiya, Peter,' he said, side-tracked at once.

Paddy-last loudly asked, 'Aengus, were you ever scared?'

'Sure,' said Aengus, struggling with Lizzie over who would lift the cousin out. 'I'm always scared you're going to turn coward at the last minute, and be the ruin of us all.'

'Are you coming?' Robbie looked in to ask. He snatched Peter from Aengus and Lizzie. 'Hurry on,' he said, vanishing downstairs.

They got through breakfast promptly. Aengus even ate his hated porridge, not wanting to waste a second in trying to avoid it.

'Great explorers,' he consoled himself, 'have to eat worse, when they're starving in the desert wastes, or being polite to savages. Sheep eyes and bugs and snakes.'

'How cruel,' said Lizzie. 'I wouldn't eat the lowest fly, to please the most civilized savage.'

'Let's get on,' Robbie urged. 'We have a lot to do, and maybe Torkeel will try to stop us. I can't wait!'

'I can,' said Paddy. 'Were you ever scared, Robbie?'

'Of course,' said Robbie. 'That's the whole point.'

They went out into the back garden, Paddy-last chirping, 'What point?' like some new species of bird. His brothers and sister were too busy settling Peter into a traffic jam to shut him up with an answer. They showed the infant how to get the most out of the squeaky bus, the tipper lorry, and the racing car, before retreating a safe distance away. Pocket awaited them on the ivied stone bench.

The shade of the three healthy sycamores blurred a lot of Pocket's defects, and gave shape to her wan face.

Still, enthroned as she was, Pocket could only inspire the most determined adventurers.

Lizzie, looking her over, asked, 'Do you think you'll ever turn as beautiful as you used to be? In books, there's always pages and pages written on how gorgeous the distressed damsel is.'

'I always skip those parts,' said Aengus.

'She's all right,' said Robbie. 'Let's get down to business.'

'She is funny-looking, though,' Paddy-last said. 'Maybe Eoin Whitehand won't recognize her and let her into Brunabawn, after all our trouble.'

Pocket said grandly, 'You children of mankind set your sights too low, who would be satisfied with the mere appearance of beauty. The noble chieftain of Brunabawn is not so blind.'

'Let's get down to business,' Robbie repeated.

Pocket continued, 'There are many beauties hidden to mortal sight, recognized only by those who know their true names. The fields you call to labour, we rouse to glory. Those ways you trod down with toil, we lift up to song. We see from within, you from without.'

'True names,' said Aengus. 'Will you tell me some of them, before we get, I mean, rescue you? For my map. I'll never get a chance like this again.' He opened his log book and poised his pencil.

'You're crazy,' Robbie said. 'This isn't the time. We have to settle my plan and everything.'

'There is time,' Aengus said. 'We can't do a thing, until moonrise. The door won't open until then.'

Paddy-last said, 'If it opens at all. We haven't got the key, have we?'

'The key's inside, silly,' Robbie said.

But his words were drowned by Pocket's indignant cry: 'Key! The door of Brunabawn was ever open. What! Does the mighty Eoin Whitehand with his noble clan, skulk like men behind locked doors?'

'Read that,' Aengus said, shoving the log book at her. 'It says, "*Within the bright key burns*" doesn't it?'

But Pocket wouldn't look. 'Some miserable detail of the mortal spell,' she dismissed it, 'of a speller wild with wits astray and magic wandering. The door, if it opens not to the moon, shall widely welcome my name.'

'I bet it won't,' said Paddy-last. 'The spell was right about everything else, wasn't it? And I don't see what good your real name is, if the only ones that know it are inside. You don't care if we sneak up on your old glacial deposit and can't get the door open while that creepy Greybranch and Torkeel tries to magic us away. You don't care. You call Lizzie "friend" but don't be her friend, or let me have the wishes I wanted, and Aengus can't even hear some silly old names for his map that you tidied away. What's in it for you?' he asked Robbie. 'You never minded Brunabawn's door before. Why do you now? Why do we have to?'

'What's wrong with you?' Robbie asked in return.

'A whole magic army chased us,' said Paddy-last. 'We're not magic. We're only kids. I get scared. I can be a hero, too, when we talk about it, but really it's scary and then I know I won't be a hero that survives for the happy ending, only a friend or relative that doesn't. Let sleeping hills lie,' he finished, the rising sobs taking him by the throat.

Lizzie sat down next to Aengus, resigning the

problem to Robbie. Robbie looked at Pocket, who stared at Paddy-last with useless fascination. *Did she think he was some strange animal?* Robbie thought with irritation.

'Listen, Padders,' he began.

'No,' Paddy ferociously refused. 'I played along and beed a hero and I'm still scared and I know something bad's going to happen. And it always happens to me.'

Robbie reasoned, 'You did as well as any of us. We were all scared when Torkeel chased us last night. We'll all be scared when we go out to open the door. Only, we're bringing weapons. The cow-driving sticks, and my sword, and anything you like, Padders. Until we get Brunabawn open, Torkeel's not going to let us alone.'

'It's her, not us they want,' Paddy-last wept. 'Why should we care about her? She doesn't care about us, does she, only to use us.'

'Look at me,' Pocket said suddenly. 'Look at me.' She swayed forward on her perch, like a fantastic scarecrow. Her voice took on an especially vibrant tone, as though to cut Paddy loose from the bonds of fear with a piercing note.

Paddy-last, hiccupping, looked.

'I will hear you sing,' she said, pinning him with her stare. 'Come, sing. There is a song within you. I hear the beat of its wings. Sing. You are he who puts words to song. Prove yourself!'

Robbie, Aengus, and Lizzie moved uneasily. They didn't like the way Pocket seemed to cast a spell on their little brother.

Paddy-last said, 'Don't have to,' and sang:

'The land is gone to sleep,
And probably won't awake.

'Cause no one knows what names to call
To rouse the hills and the fields and all:
The land is gone to sleep.'

Pocket instantly took up the tune. She sang:

'For every name that's lost
A tale is gone before.
But none can tell what the legends told
To give the names in the days of old:
The land in dreaming sleeps.'

The effect of her song took even Lizzie by surprise,
and quite undid Paddy-last's every fear. It was exactly
the magic he needed, a real and living song, that drew a
real and living vision, a dreaming shade of the glorious
past, through which the actual back garden shone flat
and dull.

How could the magic summoned by Pocket's music
be described? She herself could not guess the impact it
made on the children; on Robbie, who saw all his ideals
of glory and heroism take shape and colour; on Aengus,
who beheld the scope of that ink and paper map he
attempted; on Lizzie, who realized at a glance how
much deeper and greater was wild friendship than she
had imagined; on Paddy-last, most of all, who let himself
be drawn up into the centre of the colourful melody.

In a way, it was terrible, too. The children saw their
old familiar neighbourhood transformed into some
place dangerously beautiful. Even the old Tobervalley
Road, which had never been more than the way to and
from school, became the highway of a glittering procession, while the fields of barley and wheat, all the
cattle-dotted meadows, blazed out a vision of fey

festivities, battles, and legends. The vague rumours which young Mr MacAdam called superstition, became the blossoming, singing, growing core of a living land. All was changed by the one verse of song.

'Do it again,' Paddy-last begged of Pocket.

'Do, please do,' Aengus and Lizzie chorused.

'We haven't finished looking,' Robbie explained.

Pocket was pleased that the silliest of her magic powers, and the only one she could still command, should move these wayward adventurers so. If they could but see the fullness of her lost self!

'You see, then,' she said, acknowledging their praise, 'what Torkeel would bind forever. The stillness of shadowed woodlands was ever their song, No-song their anthem, and shall be for all, do they capture me and triumph at last.'

'Do it again,' was all the four would say.

'No, no,' Pocket shook her dusty head. 'Shall we amuse ourselves with dreams, while the hills in sleep are at the mercy of Torkeel? Let you to arms, to music go. With singing staves, defy the foe!'

'That's right,' Paddy-last agreed breathlessly. 'We'll be part of it all, then, won't we? And when you sing about the doorkeepers, everyone will see us.'

'Oh, brilliant,' said Aengus, revising in his mind the map he had begun, to include the latest legend. 'How do we do it?'

'With music,' Pocket said. 'Torkeel hates of all things, the beauty of sound.'

'Jingle sticks,' Lizzie said. 'We'll nail the bottle caps to our cow-driving sticks, and make jingle sticks.'

Paddy-last shone with delight. 'I'll get them,' he said,

127

and ran for the house, to fetch the bottle caps from under the sink.

Lizzie went for the cow-driving sticks. Robbie ran to borrow hammer and nails. Aengus went to get the phenomenon out of the way, for he'd surely, said Robbie, want to chew on the armoury.

The children ran in their various directions, while Pocket smiled with satisfaction on her throne. Paddy's brief rebellion had been a real danger, she reflected, so real that for one grey moment, she had almost imagined the presence of Greybranch's power. As though, Pocket chided herself, Greybranch would by daylight, dare the iron-gouged land.

Lizzie returned with four sticks dragging behind her. Robbie sidled out with the borrowed tools. Paddy-last was put running by his busy mother, before he could touch one bottle cap. Aengus was rooted to the ground, staring at Peter.

Everyone, even the self-centred Pocket, was finally struck by Aengus's stillness. Their steps slowed, and, when he spoke, they froze.

'Who are you? What are you? Where's our baby?'

Pocket, Robbie, and Lizzie grew cold. Paddy-last choked back a cry of terror, plummeting from the height of song to the very depths of fear.

'Where is he?' Aengus harshly demanded. 'Give him back!'

'What?' Lizzie shivered, frightened.

Robbie fiddled with the hammer, and then dropped it to take up his sword.

Pocket drew a deep, hissing breath, and wrapped her long arms all around her thin body.

Flinging aside the stick-laden Lizzie, Paddy-last scrambled to Aengus's side. He knew at once what had happened, and wasn't at all surprised to find that what looked like Peter from the back, looked like anything but Peter from the front. It was a granite face, a fixed snarl, glinting with viciously pointed teeth, and steely metallic eyes.

'Kidnappers,' Paddy-last shouted. 'Those dirty fairies stole our baby!' He turned on Pocket. 'Tricked by an old song,' he raged. 'Fooled us it was all fun.'

Robbie and Lizzie ran to see, unwilling to believe. They flinched at the hard face of the changeling, so utterly unPeterlike. Robbie raised the sword and rested its point on the pocket of the blue jumpsuit. The changeling snarled wider at contact, the rest of its horrid face was unmoving as stone.

'Get him back,' Robbie demanded, 'or I'll stick this into you. It's loaded with lightning.'

'Kill it,' Aengus urged. 'The rotten thing, cut it in half.'

'It has to tell us where he is,' Robbie said. 'Speak!' he demanded, threatening the unmoved thing.

Lizzie screamed at Pocket, 'Do something, do some of your stupid magic. They've robbed our baby.'

Paddy-last cried that Peter wasn't a hero, that he hadn't a hope, that he, Paddy-last, had always known this would happen. He hid his face on Lizzie's back, to cry without the stare of those awful bullet eyes drilling into him.

'Go on,' Aengus shouted.

'It has to tell,' Robbie shouted back.

'Do something,' Lizzie shrieked.

The changeling continued to stare, snarling.

Pocket shook herself. She stretched her arms wide. She jumped lightly from the tree stump, and skimmed across the lawn, boots dragging, until she stood by Robbie's side. Closing one bony hand over his, on the hilt of Sword Lightstriker, she pressed the blade forward. She never looked so beautiful, nor so terrible, as she did then.

It was awful to see the sword pierce the blue jumpsuit, smoking and burning into the body of the hideous rock-faced changeling. Lizzie set up a shrieking scream more piercing than the sword. Robbie tried frantically to pull back, shouting that it had to tell where Peter was, but Pocket hardly noticed him. She pressed on with dreadful intensity. Robbie's hand went numb beneath her fierce grip, and still he panted, 'Stop, it has to tell.'

When the point of the blade emerged from the changeling's back, Pocket did stop, although Aengus urged her to go on. The changeling itself snarled until its face, except for the eyes, was one mass of pointed teeth.

'Now,' said Pocket in a low voice, 'now!' and she sang, chilling even Lizzie's scream with music as icy as black waters running cold in the dark depths of a cold, cold cavern:

> 'Slink away, snarler, sneak your way to Torkeel,
> To your grey master there
> Where grey villains kneel,
> I command you, grey filth, to Greybranch reveal:
> The stolen fare better
> Than cowards who steal.'

The changeling gnashed its horrid teeth. 'The webs are woven,' it snickered. 'The nets are spread for the lamenting one of Drumanaar.'

'Go!' Pocket blazed.

'I go. I go, sorry singer,' the thing replied. It grasped the blade with its two hands and pulled itself free. 'You or the babe, you or the babe,' it said. 'We gain some poor prize.'

It went in a trail of smoke, before the children could see how or where it went. The place it had been was a patch of sticky cobwebs and grey ashes.

'Creature of snares and guile,' said Pocket, looking at the spot. 'It shall carry that scar to the end of its grey tether, a span already measured short.'

She released Robbie's hand and sword. In a weary voice, she said, 'The infant shall not be harmed. Even Torkeel has no such power. Comfort yourselves: should we fail to reclaim your child, he shall come to no harm.'

'But he isn't ours,' Lizzie exclaimed. 'We have to get him back.'

'We will, too,' Aengus vowed, 'if we have to dig up every hill in the country.'

Robbie, wringing his wrung hand, said, 'Would Eoin Whitehand get him back for us? Let's go to Brunabawn now. They can't do worse than they have. Let's get Eoin Whitehand out, to get Peter back.'

'Come on, then,' Aengus agreed.

'Get the sticks,' Lizzie shook off the clinging Paddy. 'They will be sorry they ever looked at our Peter!'

'No!' Paddy-last shouted. He, like his brothers and sister, forgot that Brunabawn could open only in moonlight. 'We don't want more fairies! Get him back

131

with your magic,' he demanded of Pocket. 'I'm not helping any fairies until we have him back.'

Pocket ferociously turned on Paddy. 'You fool! You ignorant, common child, do you suppose my magic all-powerful? The most finely wrought casket of gold cannot hold more than its fill. The mightiest nation is contained by its laws. There is no earthbound magic great or small, none in the world's knowledge, that can work all things.'

'A wish,' Paddy-last sobbed. 'We can make a wish.'

'Grey wishing is the feeblest of powers,' Pocket said with contempt. 'Did magic create out of nothing your clothes lines, bring out of nothing your bottle caps? No, nor can wishing unbind the spinners' magic of Torkeel, you foolish, stubborn child. The wonder of Brunabawn is your only hope.'

'I won't, I won't, I'm telling Mammy, she'll fix you, she'll get the police, she'll fix you all!'

Paddy-last flew into the house before anyone could prevent him. Two seconds later, barely giving Pocket time to conceal herself, Paddy was back, dragging his mother by the hand.

'He's gone, see, he's gone,' he pointed to the abandoned traffic jam of toy cars. 'The fairies got him!'

'What's going on?' their bewildered mother asked. 'Where's Peter?'

'I'm telling you!' Paddy-last stamped with temper. 'The fairies took him.'

'Hush,' said his mother. 'Robbie, what's going on?'

Robbie sheathed Sword Lightstriker, wondering what on earth to say. He could see his mother wouldn't be put off by any idle tale, she would demand to see

Peter whatever they told her. Perhaps they could get away to Brunabawn with the excuse of looking for him?

'We were just going to look,' he said as calmly as he could. 'He isn't lost. Don't mind Paddy-last, him and his fairies.'

'I'm not minding Paddy and his fairies,' his mother said angrily. 'Fetch Peter now, wherever you've hidden him. *Now.*'

She wouldn't leave them alone, so they made a pretence of searching the garden, front and back. Paddy-last raged on about the fairies, calling his brothers and sister liars: for they knew as well as he, that Peter wouldn't be found.

'Listen,' Aengus tried to tell her, 'we'll find him. Don't be worrying.'

'We'll stalk him and track him down,' Lizzie promised. 'Only we can't, when you keep following us and scaring him away.'

'Don't give me that nonsense,' their mother said. She grew angrier as she became more worried. 'Stop playing games and get Peter.'

'How can we,' Paddy-last cried, 'when the fairies have him? You have to call the police.'

After they had searched the garden ten times over, and the road, the ditches, and the fields on either side of the house, Robbie saw that his mother wasn't going to be diverted. Sickening of the uselessness of it all, he admitted, 'We don't know where he is. We thought we'd find him, without bothering you, so we didn't say straight off.'

'We would have, too,' said Aengus, 'if it wasn't for that stupid Paddy-last.'

'You don't know where he is?' Their mother's face bleached white. 'It's not a game? He's lost? Be quiet, Paddy, before I hit you!' she turned furiously on the only truthful child. 'Lizzie, run over and ask Mr Regan to help. Aengus, you go with her. Oh, but he has to be somewhere. Robbie, look in the ditch again.'

Mr Regan joined the hunt, and then Mrs Regan. The MacAdams, young and old, were roped in, and the Thompsons were called. The Grahams, the Joyces—in short, the whole neighbourhood went beating the bushes, turning the stones, raking the fields. And finally, the police were called in.

The children were by this time ordered to wait in the house, which they did gladly, still hoping to sneak away to Brunabawn. Paddy-last was unrepentant however, and refused to budge from the dining-room, where they stationed themselves. He was sure that the grownups could fix everything. They had often fixed worse.

'If you hadn't told lies,' he said, 'we'd find him. And you had better not tell the police lies, or you'll go to gaol.'

'Shut up,' Robbie fumed. 'If you hadn't opened your big fat mouth, in the first place, we'd have Peter back by now. Instead, you have to upset poor Mammy, scare all the neighbours, and waste the police's time, when they should be out catching robbers. Why didn't you be the one to get kidnapped? Wishing and kidnapping were all your ideas.'

'Look,' Lizzie called from the window. 'It's the patrol car from town. I thought it would only be Sergeant Quilty from the village.'

They all ran to see the car pull up in front of the house, with its lamp flashing on its roof.

'They'll interrogate us,' Aengus said, 'and just wait 'til they hear Paddy-last and his fairies.'

Four policemen got out of the car, and two of them came into the house, to question the children. Paddy-last got his story out first, but the smiling response so infuriated him, he gave it up at last, and retreated into the corner to sulk.

The older three patiently answered all the questions they were asked, glad that someone had finally shut Paddy-last up. They answered truthfully to: when had they noticed Peter was gone? had they heard anything? seen anyone? cries? footsteps? and had they left the garden at all? had Peter?

The last question sent Lizzie into hysterics, and the policemen decided that the children were too upset to be helpful. They promised to find the baby and went off to join the searchers.

Paddy-last shouted after them, that they had better call in the army with helicopters, and the fire brigade with ladders, for it was plain that the police hadn't a clue.

'You needn't be rude,' Lizzie said, 'as well as stupid. Did you really expect the police to believe the truth?'

Aengus said, 'Peter didn't seem lost until now, when all the grown-ups think he is. If it really was up to them, he'd never be found, would he?'

They all grew solemn at this frightful thought.

'Here's Daddy,' Lizzie reported next from her post. 'He looks sick, and there's Mammy, crying. I hope you're pleased, now, Paddy. You ought to be. You're beyond any name I can think to call you.'

'It's not my fault,' Paddy-last muttered. 'I never liked adventures.'

The afternoon dragged on, unbelievably long, as the children waited and waited in the dining-room, not knowing what was going on outdoors. Their only amusements were Lizzie's reports from the window, whenever more police or less police came, went, or stayed. Finally, the searchers outside were too scattered for Lizzie to keep an eye on, and she began gouging out a secret message on the sill. Aengus and Robbie kept an eye on the clock, and witnessed every second it marked. Paddy-last kept sulking.

The house was heavily silent, without the cries of neglected or awakened or hungry cousinhood to shatter the peace. Twice, Robbie crept upstairs to make sure that Peter wasn't, after all, asleep in his cot.

He told the others, 'I suppose the books aren't always true. In all the books I ever read, the heroes are urged by aged parents to risk their lives for glory, and not to wait at home and let the police do the deeds of valour.'

'I suppose it's an adventure for them,' Aengus said.

'They don't seem to be enjoying it,' Lizzie observed. 'But then, neither are we.'

'I'm hungry,' Paddy-last said. 'It must be way past dinner time. I'm starving.'

'How can you be hungry,' Lizzie asked, 'after all the trouble you've caused?'

'You are low, Paddy,' Aengus said.

But Robbie said, 'I'm hungry, too. If ever we do escape and get to Brunabawn, we'll want our strength.'

So he and Paddy raided the kitchen. They brought off all they could reach and carry, and faced with food, Aengus and Lizzie found their appetites.

After a pot of jam, a half-pound of cheese, a pint of milk, two apples, and a slice of bread, Paddy-last felt a lot better. The magic of Pocket's music seeped through the bored silences of the house. He began to feel a little braver, a little more willing to risk all—not for Pocket, but for Peter. Paddy-last thought of what Uncle Conor might think of someone who did nothing to rescue his only phenomenon.

He said, 'Let's do something now. Let's sneak out and go to Brunabawn, like you wanted. I don't mind. I guess Torkeel's done their worst now.'

'Stupid,' Lizzie said. 'We wouldn't get as far as the gate, without Mammy or Daddy jumping on us.'

'Why? They're not looking for us. We're not lost.'

'And they're not going to let us get lost,' said Lizzie. She began tidying the table, sweeping all the crumbs to the floor.

Aengus said slowly, 'I think Paddy's not far wrong, though. What's to stop us trying? If we could get into the ditch along the road, that would sneak us as far as the pump. Cross over to Boola, go along the hedge, and over the bog road. We could go around by Whites'. There's no one there to see us. We could go along the hedgerow behind the house, to the ruined cottages, and Brunabawn is just above them. There's plenty of cover, and so what if we're caught? We'll only be doing the good deed of looking for Peter.'

' 'Course,' said Paddy-last confidently.

'The point is,' Robbie said, 'once we're caught,

we'll never get out for another try. There are police all over the place. I'd rather wait until they're gone.'

'Besides,' said Lizzie, 'if Mammy and Daddy came in and found us gone, and that's just what would happen, Aengus, well, then, they'd be out looking for us, and worrying about us, as well as Peter.'

'Leave a note,' Paddy-last said, 'of last requests, like in books. You're not scared, are you? I'm not. Why, if anything happens, there's plenty of policemen around to save us.'

Paddy-last was spared any reply, when their parents entered with a squad of policemen, whom they installed in the dining-room with cups of tea. The children's mother was too bothered to notice the remains of the hasty meal, and the police were too polite to mention it, although more than one got a jammy sleeve.

The children were banished upstairs, where they gathered in the boys' bedroom.

'Will we try it?' Aengus asked, looking out of the window. 'It's a great chance, while they're all in drinking tea.'

On the heel of his words, their father walked in.

'Well,' he said, sitting on Robbie's bed, 'any ideas?'

'No,' Robbie said. 'What do the police think?'

Their father shrugged. 'What have you been doing since?'

'Nothing,' they all answered, fidgetting, wishing he would go.

'What were you doing this morning, then? I can't understand how a baby could vanish so completely.

Surely you heard something strange? Are you positive you didn't leave the garden?'

'Certain sure,' Robbie said.

'Not even for a minute?'

'Not a second,' said Aengus. 'Cross our hearts.'

Their father sighed, and sighed again. He got up and went to look out of the window. 'It's been a funny week, anyhow, with Thompson's clothes line disappearing and reappearing the way it did, and that noise last night in the garden, and, tell me, what was it that frightened you, when you ran to Joyces'?'

'Nothing,' Robbie said, shuddering as he realized what a trail their adventure had left, for the grown-ups to suspect and puzzle over. 'We were playing fugitives, and just got scared, you know, like when you tell ghost stories or pretend there's monsters.'

'But you were chasing someone. Jack Thompson saw him.'

'That was all part of the game,' Robbie said, unconvincingly.

Their father stared at them for a moment, not believing them, not knowing what to think. Then he said, 'We're trying to contact Conor and Ina, and get them home.'

'Oh, no!' all the children said together, horrified.

'We have to. It's not a game. So if there's anything you can tell, that will help?'

No one spoke. Paddy-last had to make an effort, to keep silent. It was dawning on him, what a heroic deed it would be, to steal a march on all those searchers.

'Well,' said their father, 'there's a detective downstairs, who wants to talk to you. Come along.'

The detective was terrible, though he tried to be nice about it. He questioned them so closely, there was no room to dodge. He was most interested in Paddy-last's account, especially about the changeling, and how Robbie had held the sword. After talking to them all together, he questioned them separately, at great length, and finally, he went away as baffled as he had come. There wasn't the least evidence that anything more terrible than disappearance had happened to Peter, and the detective was sure that, had the four children been guilty, they would have thought up a better story than one of fairies and games. But he knew quite well that they were shielding someone, for they didn't behave so much frightened, as eager to get rid of him, and to get up to something.

'We're lucky he didn't arrest us straight off,' said Robbie, when they had regained the bedroom. 'He will, if Peter isn't got back soon. We're the number one suspects. We saw the victim last.'

'I feel sick,' said Aengus.

'Don't,' Lizzie comforted. 'We know that it wasn't us that took Peter, and we'll prove it, too, when we get him back, and show up that old detective.'

'The real police were nicer,' Paddy-last said. 'But I still think they should call the army and the fire brigade.'

'We'll call our own army,' Robbie said. 'Our own fire brigade, too. At least, a fire escape. Where's the famous Pocket got to, I wonder?'

'I am here,' Pocket said. 'I have been here all this day long, waiting.'

She was in the fireplace, blending with the black bricks, as she was covered with a fine coat of soot.

The children crowded around.

'We're going now,' Robbie told her. 'Have you got the door things with you?'

Pocket settled herself in the grate. 'Patience,' she said. 'You must delay now, having delayed so long before. First, our defence needs more than mere bludgeons. Array your staves with music, even as you had prepared for. Second, we shall combine our stealth with nightfall, out of sight of the light by which men search. Third, and most vital of all, 'twould be all in vain to reach the door, before the rising of the moon.'

The adventurers reeled under this reminder.

Pocket seemed pleased to have put them down. ''Twould have been no use,' she said smugly. 'Properly armed, and the proper time, as I have waited all the day long for you to realize. However, there are some hours, yet, to prepare. Your staves are in the garden. I shall summon, if I can, with song, all that is required. Such is my sorry state, I trust not my powers, or I would sing you a blaze of thrilling armour.'

They all hung in a bunch out of the window, while Pocket tried various tunes and hums, attempting to rouse the cow-driving sticks and bring them through the air. She managed three of them, and persuaded the nails to fly in a darting shower, after which she fell back exhausted.

'We'll use shoes for hammers,' Lizzie reassured her. 'You did quite well.'

'But the bottle caps,' Paddy-last said. 'They're under the kitchen sink.'

'They're under the bed,' Aengus said, pulling out one heavy bag.

Paddy-last got so excited at the sight of untold bottle caps, he could hardly settle down to making his jingle stick. He wanted a tambourine and castanets, as well, and mused on other musical uses for the bottle caps.

Nailing bottle caps to the sticks, the children felt better than they had all day. They were doing something, they told each other, something that was more than any amount of searching the searchers would ever get through. Pocket was a great comfort to them. She gave them tales, as they worked, of how Greybranch hated music, and how all Torkeel would fall back at a blow from the jingle sticks.

Meanwhile, the search outside went on so long as daylight lasted. Bloodhounds were brought in, but proved useless, as Peter hadn't walked away, leaving a trail. All the dogs did was annoy That-Cat. And the grown-ups grew more deeply worried.

The children, of course, grew more light-hearted. When their jingle sticks were complete, their mother had them down for a late but welcome meal, just the thing they wanted before setting out. She took offence at their high spirits, and finally left them to laugh at their jokes alone. She went off to play records in the sitting-room, as she always did when troubled. The house throbbed with music.

CHAPTER 8

To Brunabawn by Moonlight

The moon rose early, floating up on the fading beams of the sun and bringing with it a fine mist that softened both lights into one. The moony mists sighed through the open windows of the darkening room, where the three staves, bright with bottle caps, lay against the wall. The note of 'last requests' was ready, a white smear on Robbie's pillow. The fire escape was prepared, an indefinable lump in the dim light. Everything was ready, from the height of the moon, to the soles of the wellingtons worn against the falling damps. Only Pocket was hanging back.

Pocket was in an awful state. The waiting, once all was prepared, had brought echoes from years gone by, doubtful vibrations which Pocket neatly caught and agonized over.

'What if they recognize me not? Or worse, have forgotten my existence entirely? Would this form I now suffer kindle memory, inspire legend? Shall I be refused entry, or be accepted in kindly pity, given a welcome for, not what is, but was?'

The children tried to encourage her, only to have their earlier remarks on her appearance cast back in their faces. Even their praise for her song only made her worry, lest she be unable to summon the song to 'cleanse the door parts of all iron breath'. Her fears reduced her to the trembling wretch the children had first found in the attic.

'You understand nothing!' she cried out against the comfort they offered. 'You think only of your cousin! I was the daughter of Lisgaoth. Now what am I? A poor singer of songs to amuse mortal minds, a hummer of meagre spells. Hideous to look upon, without and within. What have the soft lights of Brunabawn to do with such as am I?'

'Shouldn't we go now?' Robbie asked.

Pocket huddled glowing in a corner, shrinking into a puddle of sickly green. 'No, no, I cannot face them,' she whined.

'Maybe you won't have to,' said Paddy-last, impatient to get going while still in courage. 'Maybe the door won't open at all.'

'Yes, the key,' Pocket seized eagerly on the excuse. 'Could the centuries have produced a key outside my ken? Let us not risk the possibility.'

'If you think,' said Aengus, 'we're going to wait another month for Peter, you'd better think again.'

Robbie said, 'The key business will work itself out. Anyhow, we can't wait, not only because of Peter, but because of Torkeel. They won't wait, you bet.'

'Pull yourself together,' Lizzie advised kindly, though she felt like shaking her wild friend to pieces.

'Ah, could I but do so!' said Pocket.

'I'll be scared in a minute,' Paddy warned.

'No, no,' Pocket shivered.

'Oh, I wish you would get on with it!' Aengus said.

He had more to say, but the need was fulfilled by his

timely wish. The trembling green glow arose from its dark corner, swayed to the window, and said sadly, 'The time is upon us: come.' She floated out into the fog.

'I hope you haven't warned any spies of us,' Lizzie said. 'Wishing now, of all times.'

Robbie said, 'You can be sure they know we're coming, anyhow. Come on.'

The three staves were thrown out into the garden, their jingling fall covered by the loud record player. The children followed down the fire escape: first Robbie, his sword hanging from his belt, then Lizzie, and last, Aengus, struggling with the unhandy Paddy. The music covered Paddy-last's crackling drop into the holly.

'You'll never make a burglar,' Aengus told him.

'Don't you call me names,' Paddy-last said, 'just 'cause I can't tell you.'

'Peace,' said Pocket, looming up beside them. 'Keep your rancour for the foe. Are you ready, all?'

'Yes,' said Lizzie, shaking her staff at the dark wet garden and thumping it with a squelch on the wet ground.

'Then hush, and I shall sing a silence upon you, to conceal the noise of our passage, as we steal invisibly through the night. A poor work, yet perhaps of some use,' she said, still sad and self-doubting, 'against all mortal ears.'

Pocket's spell of silence was low, a mere hum among the notes blaring from the house, and it was soon over in a shower of blue sparks. Lizzie asked Pocket to repeat the song, partly to see the sparkling dust again, but mostly in hopes of learning the spell. It would be so handy for sneaking silently closer to wild animal friends.

'You still play games,' Pocket sighed, 'even as you go forth into danger. Can you not awaken to this mist, which increases the daring of those who abhor daylight.'

'Don't,' Paddy-last protested, taking a fistful of Aengus's jacket. 'I'm trying to be a hero. I think I have just enough to last until we get Peter back, if we hurry.'

Robbie said, 'No amount of mist is going to hide you, anyhow. I'm sure you can be seen a mile off, glowing like that. Can't you turn it off?'

'I shall conceal myself in our good friend's pocket,' Pocket replied. 'For the last time, a pocket shall quench my lights.'

'Then let's go,' Aengus urged. 'We haven't got all night.' He was on fire to follow his planned route, as well as get his natural phenomenon back.

Lizzie opened the pouch on the front of her anorak, and Pocket folded her long arms and legs within. She dithered a moment over the high-laced boots, doubting they were worthy of Lisgaoth's daughter. And in the end, she abandoned them. Robbie shoved them out of sight among the holly, in case the police should think they were a clue.

They crept on all fours through the hawthorn, climbed the side wall of the front garden, and dropped into the ditch. All the weapons got horribly in the way, while they were creeping, but once in the ditch, the heft of the staff or sword was a great solace. The ditch was blackly dark and wet.

146

As navigator, Aengus led, with Paddy-last hanging on behind him, fist tightly twisted into his brother's jacket. Next came Lizzie, with her pocketful, and Robbie brought up the rear, Sword Lightstriker in hand. The ditch might be perfectly dark, but it was a path that couldn't be missed, running straight with the road to just beyond the pump, where it turned in the shadow of the three elms. Aengus would lead as far as that corner, in complete concealment, after which they would climb out into open country to risk the late night search party.

'I wanted a farewell look at home,' Paddy-last complained, when the boom of the record player was finally diminished by distance. 'You're not doing it right. Heroes always take a fond farewell of their ancestral halls.'

'We're different,' Lizzie said.

'How different?' Paddy-last quavered.

Aengus told him to be quiet, and to stop hanging onto his jacket. Paddy did one, but not the other.

Little occurred on their way along the ditch, although it seemed the likeliest place for an ambush. They ran into many cobwebs, and many scratchy branches ran into them. Paddy reported something wriggling about, inside his wellington, and Lizzie asked him to save it for her museum.

Sudden noises ahead repeatedly gave Aengus pause, bumping everyone into each other. Had he not been listening for Torkeel, he would have recognized the noises at once, as the natural sounds of night. And so would have Robbie, instead of walking the entire length of the ditch backwards, his sword alert for the crackles and rustles in their wake. For a night's silent watches are the busiest hours, when insects creep, crawl, or fly forth to be hunted by hedgehogs, badgers and owls. Hundreds of mice, rats, and shrews take courage to rustle through the undergrowth. The children knew this perfectly well, having often been brought by parents or by uncles, to investigate the night, but there was no grown-up along now, nor had anyone the least thought to spare for anything but ambush. The scramble of the smallest beetle among the leaves sounded like nothing less than a cavalry charge, but the real fright was their father's voice, speaking out directly overhead.

He was in the road that ran beside the ditch, and was insisting that Sergeant Quilty come back to the house for tea, while Sergeant Quilty insisted back, that he didn't want to give trouble where there was trouble enough already. Pocket added to the insistences, as she urged the children to go on, that they couldn't be heard, that they were under a spell of silence. But the children couldn't be convinced. It seemed impossible that their father wouldn't hear. He was only a few feet away, much nearer than he had been on the night of the first fire escape. So the four children kept still, longing for the sergeant to give in and go away to a cup of tea.

Which he did, finally, remarking on how unusually wet the night was turning.

'Pocket?' Robbie whispered, struck by an awful thought. 'Torkeel couldn't have made this fog, could they?'

'Nothing so vast,' Pocket said from the pouch. 'Nothing beyond their own boundaries.'

Robbie wasn't consoled. What were Torkeel's boundaries? For they had conquered Lisgaoth, and closed

Brunabawn. Surely Torkeel considered these hills as their own hills, by right of conquest?

'Does it matter?' Aengus whispered from the front. 'Are we going on?'

'Go on,' Robbie agreed.

Secret and wet, they carried on to the end of the ditch, into the deep pool of darkness beneath the three elm trees. They climbed out there, gasping and uncomfortably warm under their wet-weather gear. By the roadside, they cowered in shadow a moment, before dashing across the road. Aengus led them full tilt into the hedge opposite, right through it into the field beyond.

'Wait,' Robbie hissed. 'I want to see if anything is following us. It will have to cross the road, if it is.'

'Okay,' said Aengus. 'There's plenty of cover here,' he added, looking with pleasure at the black bulk of surrounding blackthorn, hawthorn, and bramble.

'I'm roasted,' Lizzie gasped, plonking down on the wet grass. 'That's the worst of wet-weather gear. My feet are boiled in these boots.'

Paddy-last snuggled closer to Aengus, tightening his jacket-hold. He didn't say anything, but silently longed to go, to be away before Robbie could report a pursuer. He envied Lizzie's cool calm, her apparent ease in being able to talk about something so unimportant as being roasted. Did that mean he wasn't a hero, after all? The thought scared him. He nearly leapt right over Aengus's head, when Robbie hissed, 'All clear!'

They had only a short sprint, as far as the fork turning down to the peat bog. Lights were moving on the bog itself, and while the road to town had been empty, two cars zoomed by from the village, with their lamps blinding the children who waited to cross.

'Are they searching the bog?' Lizzie wondered. 'Do they think a heron took Peter? I suppose there are a lot of mysteries in nature, but I don't see how they could figure Peter was one of them.'

'Someone's coming,' Aengus announced.

They lay flat behind the meagre hedge, hardly daring to breathe. Pocket couldn't object, being squashed under Lizzie.

'It's only Badger,' Paddy-last sighed with relief. 'He wouldn't tell on us.'

'Shh!' the others cautioned.

Lizzie added, 'He'd think it a big joke to tell Daddy on us. And anyhow, what do you want more grown-ups for, after that detective?'

'That's what they're for,' Paddy-last began. Aengus then covered his mouth, until Badger had passed.

'Now listen,' Aengus told them all, 'we have to cross to MacAdams' garden, and jump their wall as soon as we reach it. Otherwise, any car coming along will see us at once.'

'Sure. Go on,' Robbie said.

'We know that much,' Lizzie said.

Aengus said that she knew everything, and Pocket popped up to advise, 'Peace!'

Paddy-last was jerked to his feet, as Aengus ran for the garden wall. They got over it awkwardly, as Paddy-last wouldn't give up his fistful of jacket. Robbie and Lizzie vaulted more skilfully, but even so, were nearly caught in the broad beam of a car coming from the

150

village. The swing of the headlamps' glare missed Robbie by inches.

'We're safe from the searchers now,' Robbie said. 'Everyone must be at the bog, and we're going in the opposite direction.'

'Do they know we're gone yet?' Lizzie wondered. 'I hope not. I hope they don't find out. Poor Mammy would have to climb right into the record player to get any comfort.'

Paddy-last was taking off his boot, to be rid of the museum specimen, collected in the ditch. He said, 'They won't worry, when they read the note. They'll know we're not lost. And I hope you wrote about that detective, Robbie, who—'

'It's a note, not a letter,' Robbie interrupted. 'Let's move.'

'Wait, wait!' Paddy-last struggled with his boot. But he didn't get it on in time, and had to carry it over the next wall and into the next field. Here they were in the full though fogged light of the moon, but the walls behind protected them from the searchers. Whites' house ahead was an empty threat.

Pocket poked her head out suddenly, knocking Lizzie on the chin. She said, 'Here is the dreadful scene of my captivity. Here was I first caught and made the prisoner of grey greed. Free me out, let me walk unbound to Brunabawn.'

She began kicking her way out of the anorak pouch, giving Paddy-last time to get his sodden foot back into his boot, and to regain his hold on Aengus's jacket.

'You look obvious,' Robbie said, when the glowing Pocket stood, pale green among the white mists. 'The

151

nearer we get to Brunabawn, the likelier Torkeel will be watching out and see you.'

'Mayhap,' Pocket agreed, 'yet they shall not dare cross into the cold lands, themselves, not the terrible warriors of Greybranch. No, they shall not risk their mighty powers to the iron-ploughed fields. And their minions, the p'tain, we do not fear. No, the deadly arms of Torkeel shall lie in wait beyond the hard road of the well, Tobervalley as you call the way.'

'Still, do we want them to see us coming?' Robbie asked. 'If we're going to blow our cover, if it's not blown by Aengus and his wish already, we might as well go straight across the fields and get it all over with.'

'No,' said Aengus, refusing to stray from his planned route. 'They won't see us, if we go along the hedge-row.'

'That's right,' Lizzie agreed. She felt uncomfortably alone, now that her pocket was empty. 'They won't see us until we're right among them,' she said.

'How do you know?' Robbie asked. 'They could have p'tain spying on us, right now, reporting our every move.'

Paddy-last moaned a soft protest.

Robbie went on, 'I'd like to get the worst over with. Charge into them. What do you think?' he asked Pocket.

Pocket replied, 'That you would be foolish to neglect the advice of the pathfinder. Let us hold such surprise and secrecy as is within our grasp, for so long as those weapons serve us. No warrior discards his shield until forced.'

'That's it,' Aengus said, relieved to have someone

along who was able to deal with Robbie's eagerness. 'We'll go through that gate there, and have loads of shield until we get to the road. And then we'll go around the ruined cottages to the field above, and come on Brunabawn. They won't expect us from that direction.'

'Be careful going by the cottages,' said Lizzie. 'There are swallows nesting there. It wouldn't be fair to upset innocent wildlife, that never hurt anyone, like we've bothered all the grown-ups for miles around.'

'Swallows,' Robbie snorted.

'Right,' Aengus said. 'Watch out for a wire fence ahead. We can run after that.'

They skulked along the edge of the field, rolled under the wire, and pounded for the gate. Lizzie swung it open, and they fled into the utter darkness of the hedgerow. Running felt good, after all the cautious creeping, and it was wonderful not to listen for the sneaking of ambush, to hear only the flying footfall, the thudding of heartbeats. But the path was short, and the halt at the end, sudden. Paddy-last knocked Aengus flat, causing Pocket yet again to implore, 'Peace! You must keep your rancour for the foe!'

They huddled on the edge of darkness, the Tober-valley Road broad and wide across their way, and the ruined cottages directly ahead.

No legends, ghosts, or tragedies upheld the roofless ruins that appeared as vague black lumps through the fog. The people who had once lived in them were sensibly settled in the village or town. Besides, the cottages had been thoroughly ransacked for adventure, the week before, and even Paddy-last couldn't call them scary. He had found a mug handle there, and had wished on it that wish that had been answered by Pocket instead.

The only reason they hesitated, was Pocket's warning that, from here on, Torkeel would be awaiting their arrival in full force. For the land beyond the road had never been ploughed with iron, and she wasn't sure that the spell of silence would be proof against Torkeel's greed.

'Let's run,' Aengus said. 'It's not far now.'

'Stay. Watch,' Pocket whispered.

Paddy-last settled himself comfortably against Aengus's back, prepared to wait all night.

'Why?' Robbie asked. He could see nothing but the usual clutter of abandoned stone, disguised by mist and moon.

'Oh,' Lizzie breathed. 'There is something there. In those trees around the cottages.'

'The enemy,' Pocket said, drawing back. 'See the threads of silver glisten, nets spread to capture the blind flight of dazzled wings. Small wonder such ill-conceived dwellings, those roofless walls, were abandoned by men. Henceforth, the land swells into the hills of the hidden people.'

'Superstition,' Aengus feebly protested, having heard the same from young Mr MacAdam. But he retreated with the rest, into the damp shadow, to stare and stare and blink when a glistening movement stirred in the darkness opposite. Was it the enemy, or was it the mist playing pitch and toss with the moonlight?

Aengus and Lizzie had both learned patience from long hours of observing natural phenomena. And

Paddy-last could sit still forever, to delay unpleasant-
ness. But Robbie couldn't. Once the dreaded moment
approached, he wasn't content to wait, but longed to
meet it half way.

Now, fidgetting with his sword, he said, 'Brunabawn's only up the road. Do we really have to go
through all that rigmarole, sneaking around?'

'Rigmarole?' Aengus said, offended.

'Yes. If all Torkeel's there, why don't we just run up
the road and race them to the mound?'

'All there?' Pocket said. 'Be assured, they have spared
some number of their hordes to guard the field wherein
rises Brunabawn.'

'Maybe,' Robbie said. 'So, how about if I go and see?
I'll keep behind the wall, no one will see me.'

'No, I don't like it,' Aengus said. 'There's only wire
fencing around the Brunabawn field. If we go that way,
we'd be as plain as eggs.'

'There's an ambulance phone there,' Paddy-last said,
cheering up. 'There is,' he insisted when Lizzie snig-
gered. 'It has "AA" on it, and that stands for "an
ambulance".'

'That's for cars that break down,' Lizzie told him.

Paddy-last said that cars don't need ambulances, and
Pocket advised, 'Peace' and Robbie announced, 'I'm off,
then.' He was gone before anyone could argue further.
They could hear his running feet plainly, as he thudded
away into the murky night.

'I still don't like it,' Aengus said.

Lizzie stared across at the cottages. 'Everything has to
be tried, though. Not just your route.'

'I know that. I just think we should stick together. Let

go of my jacket, Paddy-last, before you wear a hole in it. I thought you were going to be a hero.'

'I'm trying to be, but you keep saying things to scare me, and I am scared, and besides, how can I stick together, if I let go of you?'

'Heroism,' Pocket said thoughtfully, 'has indeed altered in these ages. Once, noble warriors were united in a single-minded glory, and banded together all thought, word, and deed, to smite the common foe. Time changes more than the face of the earth, I find.'

Aengus sighed, wishing to himself that Pocket would take her own advice or shut up. Fine species of a heroine she was.

Robbie hurtled suddenly into their midst. He fell among them like a gasping fish, and without waiting to catch his breath, he reported:

'They're all over the place, and there's a huge fellow under the tree at the fork of the road. He's gigantic, as tall as Daddy, at least, and he's got a shield as big as the moon, and a sword as long as a winter night, and he's just standing there like a statue made out of tin foil, watching everything—I could see his eyes shining white, watching and watching. Is he Greybranch?' Robbie turned to Pocket. 'He's got a silvery thing around his head.'

'It is he,' Pocket said. 'Lord of Torkeel.' And she drew herself up as tall as she could, a green smear of light among the black shadows. 'I shall not fly a second time,' she declared. 'Once I had a host of defenders behind me, brave Lisgaoth, bright Brunabawn. My songs were then all joyous beauty. Now they well again with hopes of freedom. I shall not fly!'

'Me, neither,' Lizzie said, vastly encouraged and forgetful that Pocket feared Brunabawn's not recognizing her, more than she could Torkeel.

'Nor me,' Aengus vowed.

Paddy-last, twisting a tighter hold on the jacket, said, 'Sure, you're not able to fly, anyhow.' He would have wished he could, if he hadn't been a hero.

Robbie said, 'Well, if you don't mind him, I won't, but there's more than him. I could see a sort of shimmer along the edges of the field, and lots of ragged banners, like cobwebs. They seem to have Brunabawn surrounded, but it's hard to tell in the mist. It's thicker up there.' He paused, and then said, 'Now let's make a plan of action and do it. I can't wait any longer. I'll go bananas. The longer we wait, the more frightened we'll get.'

'I am already,' said Paddy-last. 'Let's do something while there's a little bit of hero left in me.'

Three cars zoomed by, while the plan of action was silently considered, but no one took the slightest interest, not even in the car with flashing lights on its roof. Aengus was working out a new route, Lizzie was reviewing all her stock of stalking techniques, and Robbie imagined how it would be, if he dashed suddenly among Torkeel with his sword: could he distract them long enough for the others to get the door open?

Pocket was of the same mind as Robbie. When the third car had passed, she told the children:

'You, Swordbearer, shall challenge Greybranch and all of Torkeel with your blade of heaven's fire. What more dreadful to the hidden people than the threat of fire, the power of the storm? And I, with these the Doorkeepers, shall steal around even as our pathfinder laid down. None shall take account of us, or should a stray vigilance perceive our going, the staves of song shall beat them off.'

'Okay,' Robbie readily agreed.

'No,' and 'no,' and 'no,' said his brothers and sister. Paddy-last said, 'Daddy told me we're always to stay together, even if a monster eats one of us, the rest of us have to as well. I asked him on purpose, and that's what he told me.'

'We can't sit here all night,' Robbie said. 'Anyhow, I'm going. You can do what you like. I'm sick of creeping about, the way slugs and those p'tain do.'

'Wait,' said Pocket. 'One small protection I may give, to ease the hearts of our trio, and give them the strength to go forward without looking back. Sheathe your sword, for my poor magic will surely fall to ashes if you do not.'

Robbie obeyed, and Pocket sang low:

> 'Four into one, four out of one,
> Confusion to eyes that behold thee!
> Divide into victory
> Sally forth valiantly,
> Four into one out of one.'

She hesitated, and changed her tune:

> 'Uphold this brave messenger
> That should he in courage fall,
> His tidings will be carried through
> E'en door, e'en roof, e'en wall.'

158

She said, 'A meagre shield, but the chill of iron fades, and they may suffice. By these open skies, my magic warms to life. Would that all bloom within me once more!'

Aengus, Lizzie, and Paddy didn't heed her last words, stifling their exclamations as they saw Robbie become outlined with gold. He stood there, briefly gilt-edged, then the soft lines fell away in a dusting of light. When he stepped boldly out into the road, there were four Robbies, each drawing a sword from a sheath.

'See you at Brunabawn,' all four Robbies saluted with a sword. And they strode together away, quickly vanishing into the mist.

'Well,' Paddy-last gulped, 'maybe he hasn't stuck together, but he hasn't gone alone. So maybe it's all right.'

'Look!' Lizzie jabbed an elbow into Aengus.

They all looked, shrinking back, as the dark ruins opposite splintered with darting streaks of silver. The lights zoomed like a shower of meteors, and there emerged a grey gleaming parade of war.

They were small, but deadly, the hundreds of warriors who poured onto the road in pursuit of Robbie. The children had expected of Torkeel something mean and miserable, nothing at all like these noble, fierce faces, so unlike the p'tain, or the black-coated thief, or the changeling.

Swordsmen and spearmen, they silently flowed, grey from black shadow. The worst was to come, however, as the procession gave way to keen-eyed archers, their full quivers sparkling with deadly shafts.

'Archers,' Aengus hissed at Pocket. 'You didn't tell us.'

'They'll shoot Robbie,' Lizzie sobbed.

'They'll shoot all the Robbies,' wept Paddy-last. 'I want to go home.'

Pocket reached out a green hand to hold Paddy.

'Hush,' she commanded. 'Does the spell of protection hold true, he is safe unto the loss of his three shadows. By that, we shall have opened the door. Shall all be lost? Trust me.'

'Trust you?' Lizzie choked, watching the unending torrent of grey.

'Let me go,' Paddy-last said, pulling.

'No,' said Aengus, chewing his lip until it bled. 'We can trust Robbie, anyhow. And they won't know which Robbie to shoot. We have to go ahead and open the door, and get Peter back. It's silly to do any different. Nothing else would be any use. We just have to reach Brunabawn as fast as we can. Look, that's the last of Torkeel. Run. *Now!*'

He dashed out of hiding with Paddy-last dangling on behind, and Pocket hanging onto Paddy's arm. Lizzie had no choice but to follow.

Out of the black shelter of the hedgerow, they all felt terribly open to attack. Vague shadows loomed suddenly through the mist as they ran, ran quite heedless of thorn bushes, stumbling stones, and whipping branches. Aengus plunged them into the overgrown ruins, weeds, and trees, alive to Robbie's danger and the need for hurry. They simply had to open the door before the archers, who need not fear any amount of lightning-struck swords, could pick out the real Robbie.

They reached the field wall beyond the ruins and threw themselves over into the tall grass. Pocket darted into the lead now, as they ran ducking through the whispering stalks. She set them a cruel pace, uphill, until they came to the last gate and had Brunabawn in sight. The mound lay below them, a hump among shifting mists.

'There it is,' Lizzie wheezed triumphantly.

'Downhill to home,' Pocket hummed, excited beyond all fears. She could scarcely contain her joy. 'Oh, shall Torkeel pay dearly for all we have suffered.'

She swooped through the bars of the gate, a flurry of green light. The children were on her heels. They felt as though they were flying, soaring down from the sky to the refuge of that solid and long-sought mound. In its shadow, they all fell panting with breathless laughter.

'I knew we'd make it,' crowed Paddy-last, beating his staff jingling against the mound.

'Home is the hunter to the hill,' said Aengus.

Pocket rummaged among her skirts, murmuring, 'Oh, glorious night, may it go on forever!' as she brought forth first the Historic Doorknob, then the bell, and last the hinges.

The children became abruptly solemn, as these things appeared, dimly lit by Pocket's green glow. Then she began to sing over them, and there were changes indeed.

Pocket's true song now showed, and proved that all she had sung before had been a mere shadow of her magic. There were no words to the music she breathed over the door parts, restoring them to their former splendours. Instead, pale rainbow lights streamed from her lips, played about the knob, bell, and hinges, and took fire upon them. When she gave to Aengus the doorknob, to Lizzie the bell, and to Paddy-last the hinges, those objects burned brightly, yet cold as ice.

'We shall succeed,' Pocket whispered. 'This my true song, rekindles. Let us softly steal around, and open the door to the flooding moon, e'er Torkeel are aware of our presence. Go warily, for they surely have p'tain guarding the way. Hold ready your music and strike at once.'

'Right,' they all agreed, awed by the magic in their hands, entirely convinced that their mission would succeed.

They followed Pocket's light around the edge of the mound, through gorse, thistles, and nettles, to the eastern face of Brunabawn. There, in the misted light of the full moon, they came upon the p'tain.

Aengus and Lizzie lashed out with their jingling staves, startled into action. The p'tain were as surprised by the attack, and they fled down the field without making any defence.

'Quickly,' Pocket urged, 'for all Torkeel shall soon be roused. Plant the Opening Star, and its light shall blossom. Quickly!' she said again, as Aengus hung back in doubt.

'What? Just stick it in the ground?'

As he spoke, he saw the patch of moonlight cut out by shadow, a white square of brightness on the slope. He shoved the Historic Doorknob into the centre of the square and he reeled back when it blazed.

Pocket dragged Paddy-last from behind a lump of gorse. He threw the hinges at the blazing star, anxious to be done and to escape home. By luck or by magic, the hinges fell exactly into place. They glistened snowily by the light of the Opening Star.

Lizzie followed Paddy's example, and tossed the bell at the door. It flew in an arc of gold, and falling, seemed to catch on an invisible hook. There it hung, swinging, pealing so merrily that the children joined in, laughing and jingling their staves.

'Complete, and entire,' said a voice behind them. 'Yet locked.'

Pocket and all three children whirled around. They fell back, as they came face to face with Greybranch.

There was no mistaking so massive a figure, for any of Torkeel, even had he not worn on his brow a single colourless stone, fixed by a strand of silver. His long sword shone a dull grey, but his shield flashed as though it were freshly sliced from the full moon. Etched across its smooth surface was an intricate and beautiful design, a spider's web of purest silver. He wore armour of silver, veiled with a gossamer grey. The cloak was the only part of him that moved, wafted by the mists, as he stood just as Robbie had said, like a statue made of tin foil.

Behind him, giving the fog body, was massed all the might of Torkeel.

'Where is your key, O Daughter of Lisgaoth?' Greybranch asked, smiling at the ease of his victory. 'Lost, mayhap, or never was? Come, sing to the glories of your new kingdom, and to those who fought and waited through long ages to capture your notes.'

Pocket didn't reply, but leaned against the door, her eyes wide. The children stood between her and the grey leader of Torkeel, their staves in hand. She didn't encourage them to defend her. The huge Greybranch, triumphant and mocking, didn't silence her, but the fast-closed door did rob her entirely of speech, of song, of hope. She was but a smear of sickly green against the bright door of Brunabawn.

'You leave her alone,' Paddy-last said suddenly, startling his brother and sister. He brandished his jingling staff defiantly. 'You leave her alone or I'll hit you, you kidnapper you. The police are after you!'

Aengus and Lizzie could do no less than step forward, too, their own staves ready to strike.

A shadow gathered in the band across Greybranch's steely eyes. He asked, 'What have human kind to do with the affairs of the hidden people? Return to your cold house of stone, there is nothing for you here. Your childish mission cannot succeed, for the iron-sick magic of Lisgaoth's daughter misread the doorkeepers' spell, mistook the key. That door shall never open, nor shall the conquering might of Torkeel be diminished.'

'Won't,' croaked Aengus, determined to be as bold as Paddy-last. 'You stole our baby.'

'Yes, and Robbie,' said Lizzie. 'Where is he?'

'So there,' Paddy-last added.

Greybranch seemed to tighten into a hard and snarled knot. 'Your foolish comrades,' he said, 'lie below, struck down even in their deceit. Is this like the ransom of a babe? To steal through the mists, meddling where menkind have less right of sight, than fight? Go now, or meet an unkind fate, who would stand between the conqueror and his plunder. The White Singer is mine. As Lisgaoth in ruin collapsed, she belongs to me.'

He lunged forward, avoiding the waving sticks, and snarling through their song. All the grey mass behind him surged.

'No,' the three children shouted together.

Lizzie's staff struck the breast of a warrior, beating him back in a jangling thump. Aengus threw up his weapon to stay the fall of Greybranch's sword. They met with a searing scream. Paddy-last, treading the toes of Pocket behind him, squeezed his eyes shut, and knocked down another grey warrior.

The battle was on, a frantic last stand more confusing than anything Pocket could summon in song. Aengus met Greybranch blow for blow, while Lizzie deliberately, and Paddy, blindly, struck down the never-ending stream of Torkeel. The fog swirled thicker, pouring like milk from the moon, concealing the world from the defenders, and making them feel very alone. Mewing cries shivered the white shining air to the rhythm of jingle and thump from the ash staves. It seemed Pocket's wish was answered, that this night would go on forever.

Pocket, pressed against the immovable door, screamed, 'Make music. Blind these grey spinners with song!'

Which meant nothing to the labouring children, who could only continue to beat the jingle-thump tune of desperation. They knew that the staves winking with bottle caps could only delay their final defeat. Their arms wearied, their throats grew sore with shouting. Aengus weakened under the powerful blows of Greybranch's sword. The staves, strengthened by ash and song, withstood the onslaught unbroken. But those who wielded the jingling weapons began to crack.

Paddy-last was weakening fast. Each peek he took to see the effect of his blind warfare, discouraged and sapped his strength. He began falling back against Aengus, crowding his brother's arms. Aengus tried to keep him off, but he needed all his energy to deal with Greybranch, and he in turn began to give way, crowding Lizzie. Soon, the door and the unfortunate Pocket would be laid open to Torkeel's advance.

'Keep off, Paddy,' Aengus shouted.

'Keep off, Aengus,' cried Lizzie.

Paddy-last peeked one eye open and in panic fell back again.

Aengus and Lizzie slowly realized that the sun would rise only on a defeat. They could never hold off such an array of determined magic. Could they possibly run for it? Grab Pocket and fly for home?

Lizzie tried to signal to Aengus and missed her next blow. The staff vibrated painfully in her hand, stinging her into letting it fall. At the same time, Paddy-last's weapon went spinning up into the air.

'Get behind me,' Aengus shouted, although he felt his arms ready to fall off.

But he couldn't keep all Torkeel at bay, and at the same time meet each blow of Greybranch's sword. This was surely the end.

Suddenly, a terrific blow from behind sent Aengus, Lizzie, and Paddy-last sprawling. Pocket shot forward, thrown into the deadly arms of Greybranch. All the world leapt into brilliant light, the mists vanishing.

'There they are!' Robbie's voice sounded.

CHAPTER 9

The Key Within

As soon as Robbie had left the black shelter of darkness, he had had to struggle against a growing unease. It wasn't his mission that gave him doubts, nor the knowledge of Torkeel's massing ahead and behind. He thought perhaps the fog was the reason for his anxiety, or maybe he simply worried about his brothers and sister, left to deal with adventure, without Robbie there to organize. He moved more quickly, as though hoping to leave his uneasiness behind. But it stuck closer than the mists.

The foggy night of white and black, made up its own version of light, a shifting and deceiving revelation of looming bulks that continually gave Robbie pause. A sudden tree, grey against the fog, an abrupt pole, or a surprising road sign—they appeared like magic, and vanished like smoke, silent and without excuse.

Robbie halted before a glistening, colourless sign, that warned of the forking road ahead. His boots made no sound on the tarmac. He glanced swiftly left and right at his three spellbound companions.

They really were well done, as far as he could tell. Moving a beat or two beats, or three behind him, they each pretended an air of independence. They should fool any watchers. They had nearly fooled Robbie, too, and there he recognized at last the source of his anxiety.

The three silent images could neither give warning nor defend themselves against sudden peril, as Robbie, unthinking, had been expecting them to do. Worse, they couldn't care less, being entirely heartless as well as brainless. They weren't Aengus, or Lizzie, or Paddy-last. They weren't even Robbie. They were nothing but images reflected on the fog.

'I'm all alone,' Robbie thought, loudly it seemed, for the three images looked in his direction as though he had spoken.

'Come on, then,' Robbie said, really speaking. His voice sounded more shallow than had his thought.

He went on, passing the road sign, which quickly vanished. A clump of shrubbery loomed, then ducked hastily, like an embarrassed intruder.

A song of Paddy's kept coming to mind, and Robbie kept pushing it away.

> *Darks scuttle into corners.*
> *They slither into holes.*
> *They disguise themselves as furniture*
> *Or trees or rocks or poles.*

Robbie walked more quickly, and then broke into a run. He couldn't bear the loneliness of the fog any longer. Even the company of Torkeel in all its battle array would be more concrete a danger, than the three images were a comfort. And the sooner he faced them, of course, the sooner he would be reunited with his real companions.

He fetched up against the gate unexpectedly. The mists swirled behind him, shrouding the road, blurring the edges of the look-alikes. Robbie leaned against the cold wet bars, trying to hear something besides the thump of his heart. There was no sound, no clink of weapons, nor whispered command to attack. The fog shone faintly silver, but as blankly blind as ever.

Darks slide along without a sound,
Darks don't pretend they're there.
Darks snigger when your back is turned
And snicker when you stare.

Robbie sighed. He lifted the bar of the gate and slipped through, letting the bar close noisily. The metallic clang was pleasantly real. Squeezing the hilt of Sword Lightstriker, Robbie moved forward, into the field of Brunabawn.

One of the images glided to the fore. One moved in beside Robbie. The third followed, miming a vigilant rearguard.

Big deal, thought Robbie, keeping his eyes fixed on the one ahead, hoping it knew the way to the mound through the fog. Anyhow, something had to happen now, for good or bad. Surely Torkeel would appear and attempt to halt his advance.

A whistling shriek rent the blank night. It concluded with a thud, a surprisingly solid thud, as the black arrow struck down the leading image.

Robbie jumped back a pace, horrified to see what looked like himself, thrashing with pain. The silver fletching of the arrow flashed white, as the false Robbie rolled in agony, its face grimacing horribly. It took ages to subside.

Stillness returned, pressed down by the fog. Robbie

waited a moment longer, until his courage threatened to fail. Then he moved on, widely skirting the fallen image. The one beside him went ahead to take its place.

Robbie walked gingerly, waiting for the next arrow. When it came, screamingly sudden, he used the start it gave him to run forward rather than back. He swung Sword Lightstriker as though clearing a path for himself, and he jumped right over the stricken look-alike. The last image stayed sensibly at his side.

They hadn't run ten blind yards, when an entire chorus of shrieking arrows rushed out of the fog, silver fletching darting like knives of rain. One squelching thud brought the arrows up standing, forming a circle around Robbie and his double.

'Come out!' Robbie shouted, whirling around and around. 'Show your face, coward! You can't hide forever. Come out and fight.'

He turned the full circle, swung by the weight of Sword Lightstriker, and stopped awkwardly, unbalanced by his furious spin. He looked up, panting with anger, into the hard gaze of Greybranch.

For one frozen moment, they regarded each other wordlessly—the powerful warrior chief of Torkeel and the solitary boy. Robbie began a panic train of unspoken prayer, as he sought to regain his wits, if not his courage. Then Greybranch spoke, and Robbie felt a calm wash over him like a warm light.

Greybranch said, 'What brings you armed to Bruna-bawn?'

Robbie cleared his throat. 'What did you do that for?' He gestured back to indicate the fallen images. 'We aren't doing any harm.'

'No harm in you, child of cold hearths,' Greybranch said. 'The moon in the mists has sent your wits astray. Return to your iron-gouged lands, to your reason, to your well-being.'

'We don't own any land,' Robbie said. 'You're mistaking me for someone else. And our hearths aren't cold. We often have fires. Or is it because you're magic, that you think ordinary fire isn't hot? Lightning is a lot hotter, I suppose.'

A sigh stirred the mists. Glancing swiftly sideways, Robbie saw that he and his lone survivor were surrounded by a fierce and innumerable band. Torkeel's armour of silver and grey blended glinting with the fog, part of it: seeping and spreading over all the night, blotting out the moon. But there was only one Greybranch, tall and powerful as a legend, crowned with a thread of silver and one colourless stone.

So what, thought Robbie. *I don't have to fight them, only delay them until the door is opened.* 'Well,' he said, casually lifting his sword until it pointed at the broad chest of Greybranch. The sword trembled, and he had to support it with both hands.

'You seek the babe,' Greybranch said, getting down to business. 'I seek what is mine by right of conquest, the White Singer of Lisgaoth. You and yours have no claim upon her. Nor she upon you.'

'So?' said Robbie. 'That's all very interesting, but I don't see what it has to do with you and your arrows. It's no excuse for shooting anyone. I mean, if anyone had something belonging to me, quite by accident, like, I wouldn't sneak around stealing their babies. I'd just ask them for it back, politely.'

'Thus you,' said Greybranch, almost smiling, 'come to request the return of your infant: armed with fire, creeping through hedges, sneaking through fog to Brunabawn.'

'That's right,' said Robbie. 'So, where is he?'

To his utter astonishment, Peter came staggering into the circle of arrows. 'Wammer,' he said, grabbing Robbie about the legs.

Greybranch watched coldly, only the gossamer of his cloak moving, winking over the silver armour. Without smiling, he appeared chillingly amused at Robbie's dilemma.

Robbie said nothing, being speechless. Peter, after his one remark, plumped down onto the wet grass and chewed on his fingers. And the others? Aengus, Lizzie, and Paddy-last were very much in Robbie's mind, as he looked down upon his cousin. Had they reached the mound yet? Was he to wait here until they did?

Minutes were like hours to the lone adventurer, caught in the midst of Torkeel with a helpless baby, and a useless image, and no plan of action. He couldn't very well offer to hand over Pocket, nor could he start a fight, with Peter underfoot.

Then the whistle of an arrow pierced the mist, and the last of the look-alikes fell.

'That's not fair!' Robbie cried out.

'Your schemes are undone,' Greybranch said sternly. 'Come, strike with your fell weapon. You stand near enough, I misdoubt, to lay waste all of Torkeel.'

'So I will, too,' Robbie declared.

He lashed out, and fell over Peter, who wailed. A full wind of screaming arrows blew through the fog.

'Cowards!' Robbie shouted, tucking Peter lumpishly under one arm. He ran, stumbling through the masses of Torkeel. The warriors one and all backed off from the threat of lightning-tried wood.

Later, Robbie figured he was let go. At the time, however, he did no figuring at all. With arrows tattering the fog, with Peter wailing and wriggling under his arm, all Robbie could do was run. No bold warrior chose to meet the challenge of Sword Lightstriker, and if one had, Robbie didn't suppose there was much he could do about it. He had no intention of leaving Peter down, where anyone could take him up. After all, Peter was more than half the point of the mission.

Just when the fall of arrows ceased, Robbie couldn't tell. One moment, he was speeding among them, hands grazed but sword valiantly held aloft. The next moment, all was confusion. He seemed to at once leave the ground, to float right up into the full blaze of the moon. And at the same time, he seemed to be sinking into the earth, plunging into the damp scent of cold clay and worms. He squeezed a tighter hold on cousin and sword, and he held his breath.

*   *   *

Far above, a distant and beautifully carved ceiling glowed in a warm rainbow array. Delicate blues flickered through fragile green, pale golds shimmered by gauzy pinks. In, through, and among the gently moulded stone, the softly coloured lights blossomed like a dreaming field of flowers adrift with butterflies.

Below the garden of lights, those same colours

winked shabbily among the assortment of people. They were gathered at one end of the huge and gorgeously lit hall, and they all stood facing, and in fact gaping at, Robbie and Peter.

Robbie carefully placed Peter between his feet, where he could keep a sort of hold on him. He held his sword ready and looked all around.

The dully shining crowd made no move, but stared fixedly at Sword Lightstriker.

'Where am I?' Robbie asked, having taken in the hall, the tapestries, that hung dustily along its length, and the respectful stillness of the gathering.

Peter squealed, and Robbie told him to shut up. Then he repeated his question.

' 'Ware, stormlights,' someone in the crowd murmured, as the assembly rippled, bright eyes flashing to converge on one figure who stepped out from the crush. He was nearly as tall as Greybranch, Robbie thought, but rather starved looking. He was clad in a pearly white that shone with faint iridescence. He ignored, or didn't acknowledge the warning, but came on to stand directly in front of Robbie.

'Who are you?' Robbie asked.

'You are the stranger,' was the answer, politely but firmly given. 'You declare yourself, and the message which carried you through roof and wall, into this doorless hall.'

'Message? Shut up, Peter! I don't have any message.'

This puzzled the questioner, who frowned in a bewildered way, saying nothing.

Robbie looked beyond, at the clutter of people, to the end of the hall. The men there were armed with swords, the ladies with jewelled bows and daggers. But they seemed harmless enough. Beyond them again, was a blank darkness, as though the bright chamber had not quite made up its mind how to finish.

His attention was brought back to the white-clad leader, who now asked, 'Explain, then, the token of that spell which brought you here, which even by the fierce flame of your sword cannot be broken. If you have passed through dreadful perils to this hall, your reticence is understood, yet not forever excused. Say, I command, what errand sends two mortals within the walls of Brunabawn?'

Robbie lowered his sword, which was instantly grabbed by Peter. 'Brunabawn?' Robbie gulped. 'I'm in Brunabawn? But that—' A wave of panic swept over him, receded and threatened to beat again. Robbie hated underground sorts of places, whether they were cramped tunnels or vast doorless halls.

'Say on,' said the leader.

Robbie made a huge effort to control his fear. He looked up to the ceiling with its lights, he looked down the hall at the well-worn company. He brought his gaze back to the leader.

'You're Eoin Whitehand,' he said. 'All right. Listen, Pocket put a spell on me, that must have got me this far, a second spell I forgot about. All right, then, listen: she's out there with my brothers and sister, trying to open the door. See? And Torkeel and Greybranch, of course, are out there, too. We have to get out before they're caught.'

Despite his efforts, Robbie's last word squeaked.

Eoin Whitehand hadn't a clue what Robbie was

talking about. 'You speak in riddles,' he said. 'Who is this Pocket? What claim has she, with your brothers and sister, upon Brunabawn?'

Robbie took a deep breath. He pulled at Sword Lightstriker, but Peter hung on.

'Listen,' he said, 'I can't tell the whole story now, there isn't time. We have to get out of here. See,' Robbie said, gabbling rather, 'when Greybranch and Torkeel stole your door, this fellow, speller Joyce, put a spell on it, so that when Pocket got free she could put it together, with us helping her. She says it's a mess of a spell, I don't know why, but maybe it is, or they'd be here by now, but anyhow, it was the only spell there was, and her own spells aren't so hot, either. The only thing she can do well is sing.'

'Sing?' Eoin Whitehand cried out.

Robbie hadn't thought that the crowd had been making any sound, but they must have done, for a sudden and intense silence fell hard on the heels of Eoin Whitehand's exclamation. The many bright eyes watched Robbie with precious hope.

'Yes, she sings,' Robbie said. 'But you must know all about that. She's Lisgaoth's daughter.'

The silence was profound, and, Robbie suspected, unbelieving.

'It's all true, I promise, but she can't remember her proper name, on account of all the pockets she was in. And I guess she looks different from what she used to. But she really is Lisgaoth's daughter. She recognized the doorknob straight off, and the bell and the hinges, and Torkeel is out there now, trying to capture her, and if we don't get out and help, I don't know what's going to happen.'

'Amfranbán!' Eoin Whitehand said. He turned to face the rustling, bright-eyed and shabbily clothed crowd. 'Amfranbán, painter of songs, the weaver of singing tapestries! Dark are the glowing halls of Brunabawn, deep in the dust of disharmony, without the songs of Amfranbán.'

While he and his court exchanged glad exclamations, Robbie struggled with Peter for possession of Sword Lightstriker. Peter had the advantage of his mouth, plus his two hands. Robbie's hands were clammy and damp, and Robbie wasn't in his most valiant form, anyhow. The foggy, lonely walk, the confrontation with Grey-branch, and now the ordeal of being trapped underground, sapped his adventurous valour. At that moment, he wanted nothing so much as to get safely home, and to spend a few blameless weeks doing something useful, like building model ships, or reading, or nothing at all.

The company of Brunabawn finished their congratulations, scattered, and disappeared behind the many tapestries.

Eoin Whitehand turned, beaming, to Robbie. 'We prepare for battle,' he said, 'inspired by your brave tidings. We shall not long delay, be at ease in that, for we who have longed for ages to enjoy again the dewy freedoms of moonlit nights, cannot be less eager than are you, to quit this glorious prison. Then shall we burst forth upon Torkeel, rending their grey weavings, shredding their grey spells.'

'Okay,' said Robbie. 'I'll wait here.'

Eoin Whitehand bowed and left the hall.

Alone but for Peter, Robbie restrained himself from

running in panic around the hall. He could hear a rustling, a ringing of preparation. No doubt all those keen-eyed people were glad and eager to help, but Robbie would have given the lot for Aengus, Lizzie and Paddy-last.

'So I'm left with you,' he said, wresting the sword from Peter. 'Here's your chance to prove yourself a true comrade in arms.'

Peter whined and began crying for the sword.

To calm his own fears, as well as shut up Peter, Robbie took up the infant and brought him on a tour of the hall, going from tapestry to tapestry. He read to Peter the tales stitched there in gold, silver, and precious stones. They passed through battles, festivals, and royal ceremonies, and paused over the slaying of a dragon. Peter subsided into a sleepy whine, as Robbie lectured on dragons. And after the blazingly woven monster, they moved on to meet a blank wall.

Robbie leaned against the cold stone. All the weight of underground-ness returned like an avalanche. Peter jigged about, trying for freedom, heedless of his cousin's awful state.

'Once the door of Brunabawn,' Eoin Whitehand said. 'And shall be again.'

Robbie looked up to find Brunabawn's chief arrayed for battle. He shone brilliantly, all shimmering colours in white. Behind him, the nobles of Brunabawn crowded like a shoal of fallen stars. This was more like it, Robbie thought, stirred by the sight.

'They should be here by now,' Robbie said, turning to the cold bare stone. 'I hope they're okay.'

A sharp crack! sounded in reply, causing all the

assembly to gasp. There followed a sighing whisper of song, a distant whine of bells, which made Peter laugh.

Everyone pressed forward to see the outline that sprang brightly from the bare rock. It was as though a blinding light shone beyond, forcing the cracks between door and jamb.

Eoin Whitehand unsheathed his sword, as did all of his company. The air sang. The tall leader reached out to open the door.

It wouldn't budge.

He threw his shoulder against the door, his armour ringing loudly as it struck.

The door was unmoved.

'Oh,' said Robbie then. 'The key—the door's locked.'

'Locked!' said Eoin Whitehand furiously.

The company echoed his indignant cry.

'That's what the instructions said,' Robbie defended himself, blushing under the angry eyes that were fixed on his face. 'Pocket would say it wasn't so. I thought she knew what she was talking about, or that you'd have the key, if there was one.'

'Are we men,' Eoin Whitehand raged, 'to skulk behind locked doors?' He pounded the shining outline, calling, 'Amfranbán!'

The warriors behind him, afire for battle and inflamed by the check, began muttering abuse of Robbie: a muddled mortal; crazed by the moon; and even, a trick of Torkeel's, to penetrate our defences with that flaming sword. Robbie was embarrassed and felt guilty, at first. Then a rising anger overtook these emotions. He began to fling back their insults, and the hall rang with angry shouts. Above them all, the voice of Eoin Whitehand called to Amfranbán.

The turmoil grew louder, the threats more dangerous. Robbie awkwardly lifted his own sword, with Peter wriggling for release, as several warriors appeared ready to do battle then and there. The sight of the fire-tried blade silenced the whole company. Even Eoin Whitehand drew back from the Sword Lightstriker raised in anger.

Eoin Whitehand said softly, 'Sheathe your sword, and let us take counsel.'

'Won't,' Robbie said. He could be as stubbornly unreasonable as Paddy-last, when pressed. 'Make me. I went through all Torkeel, even Greybranch, to get here, and now you call me foul names. My brothers and sister are creeping about in the dark because of you and you act like I'm some low traitor. My cousin was kidnapped, and you're all waiting for the chance to stab me with your swords. Pocket's always telling us that heroes were different from what they are now, and I guess she's right: if you were ever heroes at all!'

'Wam!' Peter roared in complete accord. He grabbed at the sword, wriggled, and tumbled down. Robbie, quite unthinking, let go of his fell weapon, trying to catch Peter, but he wasn't half quick enough. There was a confusion of stirred colours, an intake of many breaths. The next thing Robbie saw was Peter darting among the company, making all give way to his fiery advance, Sword Lightstriker aloft.

Robbie couldn't help but laugh, as Peter staggered chuckling among the heroic gems of Brunabawn, thrashing the air with the silver-painted wood. The nobles heaved and shifted in dreadful respect for that unquenchable fire which only those who fear it can see.

'Bind him!' Eoin Whitehand furiously commanded Robbie. 'You court your own undoing!'

Robbie didn't answer, helpless with laughter.

In a rage, Eoin Whitehand pushed Robbie aside, to hammer uselessly at the locked door. The blows rang out deafeningly, drowning the noise of Peter's charge, of Robbie's mirth. It seemed impossible that anything could withstand such an onslaught, but the door held.

'Hermperdem?' Peter swung around, attracted by the din. Then he took off, homing in on the thunder like an errant streak of lightning.

' 'Ware sword!' cried out all of Brunabawn, parting to let the fiery phenomenon through.

Peter aimed straight for Eoin Whitehand.

Robbie was shocked enough to cry out. Eoin White-hand moved just in time, and Peter ran full tilt into the door.

Instantly, the door exploded outwards. A cold wave of moonlit fog poured in. Beyond, the silver bulk of Greybranch and of all Torkeel loomed.

'There they are!' Robbie shouted, as he tackled Peter.

CHAPTER 10

Amfranbán

When the rush was over and all of Brunabawn had joined battle with Torkeel, Robbie picked himself and Peter up. He sheathed Sword Lightstriker, and hauled on Peter, and walked out into the damp chilly night.

This was marvellous, he thought, taking great lungfuls of free, foggy air. More splendid than any amount of tapestried halls, however well lit.

'Formerlap,' Peter moaned, pointing.

Robbie looked down the field, where flashes of ferocious fighting lit the fog. It seemed as remote as history.

'That's not for us,' he told Peter. 'We've done our bit. We'll find the others and go home.'

He hoisted Peter onto his shoulders. The infant automatically grabbed painful hold of Robbie's ears, but Robbie didn't mind. Grasping the two baby feet, he turned his back on the battle and laboured uphill to the top of the mound. He softly called the names of his brothers and sister, hoping that they weren't so madly adventurous as to have joined in the fighting. Peter called as well, dribbling into Robbie's hair.

'Robbie?' Paddy-last's voice sounded, snuffling from the shadows. A black figure detached itself, and nearly threw Robbie to the ground. 'My jingle stick!' sobbed Paddy-last. 'I lost it!'

'Robbie!' came Aengus's voice.

'And Peter!' Lizzie rose up from the clumps of gorse.

It was as glad a reunion as ever was, on a misted fairy hill in the middle of the night, with hoards of ferocious warriors in fierce contention below. They thumped each other, more gently than did the heroes in the field, and they exchanged wisps of interruptions and generally agreed that the one thing left to do, was to go home.

They none of them had the least interest in the battle. If they'd considered it, they would have simply shrugged, 'Brunabawn will win,' because after all they had been through, Brunabawn couldn't do less. But the children didn't consider, and neither did it make any claim on their attentions.

'So, let's go,' Robbie said. 'After all, we can talk it over tomorrow, or the next day, or whenever we like.'

'Let's,' Paddy-last agreed feverishly. 'There's plenty of bottle caps left at home, for a new jingle stick.'

'This way,' Aengus directed them. 'We don't want to walk through the battle.'

They started down the far side of the mound, to return by the round-about route the Doorkeepers had earlier arrived by, in the company of Pocket. No one interfered with them. By the time they reached the gate into the next field, the battle was entirely hidden. Only the mound showed faintly outlined in silver.

'What happened to Pocket, anyhow?' Robbie asked, pausing to look back. 'Did I tell you her real name?'

Lizzie said, 'When Eoin Whitehand came out, Grey-branch flung her aside. I didn't get the chance to see whether she turned beautiful or not. I suppose I never will.'

'I didn't think,' said Aengus, leading the way to the ruined cottages, 'that you cared what your wild friends looked like. You wouldn't have any, if you did.'

'She wasn't really my friend,' Lizzie said. 'It was just a name, like being Honorary Treasurer, without any treasure to honour. It didn't mean anything special.'

'Never mind,' Paddy-last hiccupped. 'Uncle Fergus says, there's always plenty more snakes in the grass.'

Peter said, 'Dadada.'

Robbie said, 'Ouch.'

They got over the wall awkwardly. Ducking and stumbling among the ruined cottages was more difficult, when taken slowly. No one minded: they were going home.

They reached the road with relief.

'I'm worn out,' said Paddy-last. 'Maybe we'll meet a car that will give us a lift.'

'It would be a squad car,' said Aengus, 'at this time of night or morning. We'll stick to the road, will we? Now that we have Peter, no one can arrest us for anything.'

'We ought to get medals,' Robbie said.

They went on, boots scuffling, Peter breathing remarks into Robbie's ear. They had to watch carefully for the turn in the road, the fog still being heavy.

'By the way,' Lizzie said, 'what was her real name?'

Robbie said, 'Amfranbán,' just as Aengus said, 'Here's the turn,' but neither was heard. As they spoke, an eruption of white light shot up, severing the darkness.

It came from the well, a deep but muddy pool much tramped by cattle, and overhung with a thick canopy of leaves. The muddy hoof prints showed stark, and the undersides of thousands of leaves shone bright as day, in the uprush of brilliant white sparks. It was millions of stars rushing to the sky, it was millions of sun-soaked raindrops running for home.

The children fell back, staggered by this unexpected leftover from their adventure. Shielding their eyes, they peered into the white glare.

'Amfranbán,' Peter said plainly. It was the sort of thing he would and could say.

Amfranbán turned in the midst of the fountain. She swept her arms upwards and the light grew, if it were possible, more brilliant again. Still, they could see her, blinding though she was. She smiled at them.

She didn't speak at all, yet they all understood the meaning of her smile, of the upraised arms, of the shake of her head: they had unlocked a spell worked by the merest amateur, a spell so muddled, that even Torkeel had been baffled by its meanderings. With all her brightness, Amfranbán thanked them.

The children smiled back, delighted with their own cleverness, delighted to have their talents recognized.

Amfranbán swept up another great splash of light and rose. The fog suddenly vanished. The moon flashed out in its full golden glory, far to the west. In the east, the sky gleamed with a rising dawn.

The brilliance of the well streamed away, leaving Amfranbán alone in her own white light. Her silver hair rippled, her eyes sparkled green, and in each of her hands, she held a rainbow.

Then she, too, streamed away. She was gone before the first finger of day reached out to dim the moon.

'Wow,' Paddy-last breathed, staring into the shadowed and mucky well.

Robbie tried to arrange Peter more comfortably on his shoulders, but Peter resisted.

Aengus made a move towards the dirty water hole.

'Listen!' Lizzie said, grabbing his arm.

They all listened. One bird sang out a solitary note, and on the wings of its call came another, drifting soft-feathered down the dawn breeze:

> 'The hills turn in green sleep
> A dreaming song they give.
> With every dawn the music flares,
> With those who hear
> Their bright songs they share.
> The hills in dreaming sleep.'

'Do you know what time it is?' a sarcastic voice asked behind them.

The children started violently. Robbie nearly let Peter fall. They turned to look into the face of a policeman, who was leaning out of a car window.

Aengus said, 'Must be nearly six.'

'Time you were home?' a second policeman suggested, craning within the car to get a look at them.

The children shuffled their feet, feeling guilty. Lizzie wondered should she dare ask for a lift. But perhaps policemen weren't allowed to give lifts.

'Come on,' the first policeman said, solving her problem. He reached behind to open the back door. 'That's the lot of you, is it?'

'It's plenty,' the second policeman said, as they all tumbled in. 'I'd pity them, if they weren't the cause of our being out all night. Where do you suppose they were?'

'Dancing with the fairies,' the sarcastic policeman said bitterly. 'What else?'

The children, excepting Peter, heard not a word of this. Before the car moved off, they were sound asleep.

Peter, however, had seldom been so lively. He clambered over his cousins until he could comfortably stand on Paddy's stomach, and get a good view out of the rear window.

'Amfranbán,' he murmured.

And he set about chewing holes in the upholstery.

THE END